# Tales of
# KING ARTHUR

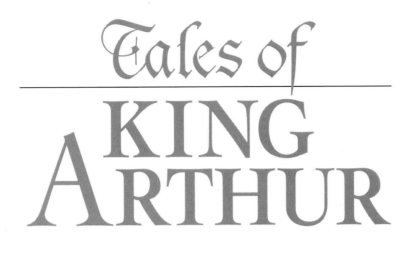

# Tales of
# KING
# ARTHUR

RETOLD BY DANIEL RANDALL AND RONNE RANDALL
ILLUSTRATED BY GRAHAM HOWELLS

ARMADILLO

Published by Armadillo Books
an imprint of
Bookmart Limited
Registered Number 2372865
Trading as Bookmart Limited
Desford Road
Enderby
Leicester
LE19 4AD

ISBN 1-84322-067-9

Produced for Bookmart Limited by Nicola Baxter
PO Box 215
Framingham Earl
Norwich  Norfolk  NR14 7UR

Designer: Amanda Hawkes
Production designer: Amy Barton

Printed in Singapore

# CONTENTS

# INTRODUCTION

The legends of King Arthur are among the richest and most mysterious in British folklore. Besides being exciting stories, they deal with important and timeless themes such as justice and the struggle for power.

There almost certainly was a real leader named Arthur, but he was probably not High King of all Britain. The Celtic people were still living in clans, and the rivalries between these clans were so deep that it was unlikely they would have chosen one king to rule over them all. In his legendary role as Pendragon, Arthur represents the ideal of unity, something many Celts may have wanted, but never really achieved.

The hero we know as King Arthur was probably a clan chieftain who most likely came from Cornwall, Wales, or Scotland, and lived between AD 450 and 530, not long after the end of Roman rule in Britain. He used tactical and military skills learned from the Romans to ward off Saxon invaders. His most important recorded victory was at Mount Badon, where one account says he killed 926 men single-handedly. This probably isn't accurate, but it tells us that he was a skilled and much-admired warrior.

Tales of Arthur's deeds spread throughout Britain, and in the 1100s the bishop Geoffrey of Monmouth recorded his version of the Arthur legends in his book *The History of the Kings of Britain*. The stories spread across the sea to France, where, in the twelfth and thirteenth centuries, poets like Chrétien de Troyes added to the legends by introducing romantic characters, such as Lancelot.

Since then, countless poets, historians, playwrights, and, more recently, filmmakers have added their own versions of the Arthurian legend. It can be difficult to find one's way through all these stories to the true Arthur at their heart. But one thing is not difficult to find—the richness of the legends, and of the messages they carry. The stories of this fiery Celtic warrior echo through the ages, making him a hero for all time.

# PROLOGUE

When the Romans came to Britain, Rome was a mighty empire, whose rule extended over much of the known world. Britain, an island standing alone in northwestern Europe, was to be its final northern frontier. The land was green and fertile, with valuable resources to be mined in its hills. Emperor Claudius conquered the island in AD 43, and Britain remained part of Rome for more than three hundred years.

But with time, the might of the Roman Empire crumbled, and it began losing territories. Britain was one of them. Menaced by native tribes and by Saxons across the sea, the Romans knew their time in Britain was coming to an end. Gradually, they began sailing for home, leaving Britain in chaos.

The native peoples of Britain fought with each other. Those who had taken up Christianity, the new religion of Rome, warred against those who had stayed true to the Celtic religion. Tribes from the north made raiding trips south, and Saxon tribes from across the sea were a constant threat.

A land that had once flourished was being torn apart. It had been plunged into darkness, and few could see the light.

But out of the darkness came hope, in the form of a great man, a man who would heal the rifts that had split his country, and unite his people. He would drive the invaders back, and make Britain whole again.

The story of this extraordinary man and his deeds lived on long after he was gone, and spread throughout the world. It is the story of King Arthur, and there is magic in its telling.

# UTHER AND IGRAINE

It was a troubled time for the island of Britain. The Romans had left, and now the Celts battled viciously among themselves. Britain and her people were being destroyed.

A warrior named Uther showed great bravery and skill in these wars, and he soon rose to become Pendragon, High King of all Britain. He knew that his first task must be to unite his kingdom by getting the warring chieftains to join together under his leadership.

Uther Pendragon could be hot-tempered and thoughtless, so he asked his most trusted advisor, Merlin, to help him. Merlin was a Druid, a Celtic priest, and some said he could do magic. His wisdom, understanding, and gentle spirit would help Uther convince the chieftains to join with him and make peace, not war.

One of the first people Uther and Merlin went to see was Gorlois, the lord of Cornwall, in his castle at Tintagel. Gorlois was a good and reasonable man, and he soon agreed to accept Uther's leadership. When their talks were over, Gorlois prepared a huge feast for Uther and his men.

During the feast, Uther looked up, and, across the table, saw the most beautiful woman he had ever laid eyes on.

"Who is that?" Uther asked Merlin.

"That is Igraine, Gorlois's wife," the old man answered.

Uther said nothing, but Merlin saw Uther's eyes gleam just as they did when he was in battle. To Merlin, this could only signal trouble.

Later in the evening, Uther spoke to Merlin again. "I am in love with Igraine!" he whispered. "I must have her for my wife!"

"She is married to Gorlois!" Merlin whispered harshly. "She cannot be yours." But even Merlin knew that it was no use. Once Uther's mind was made up, no one, not even Merlin the Druid, could change it.

Uther left the castle that night, but at daybreak he laid siege to Gorlois's castle in an attempt to steal his lands—and his wife. In the midst of the fighting, Merlin found Uther on his steed, watching the battle from a rocky outcrop.

"What makes you think," Merlin said slowly, "that Igraine will want to marry you after you have killed her husband?"

"I think," replied Uther, smiling, "that she will not know he is dead."

Merlin shook his wise old head. He knew exactly what Uther had in mind, and he knew how determined Uther was.

"I will help you," sighed Merlin, "but only this once. And you must do something for me in return."

"I will do whatever you ask," Uther promised.

"At nightfall," said Merlin, "I will make an enchantment that will turn you into Gorlois. Igraine will welcome you as her husband."

"And what must I do in return?" asked Uther.

"Only this," Merlin replied. "When your son is born, you must give him to me."

Uther turned pale. "You ask a high price for your magic, Merlin," he said.

"Yes," said Merlin, "and you must swear to pay it."

"I swear it," said Uther quietly. "I swear it as your High King."

The battle raged on through the day, neither side gaining the upper hand. As the sun set, Gorlois heard that Uther had retreated.

"We must pursue him!" he cried. He saddled his horse, and rode with twenty of his men out into the darkness.

On the outcrop, Merlin was beginning his enchantment. As he mumbled ancient Celtic spells, a mist began to creep in from the sea. It rose higher and higher, like smoke from a dragon's nose. It encased Uther, and then, as Merlin thrust his staff into a soft patch of earth, it receded and left the two men standing on the outcrop.

But it was no longer Uther who stood before Merlin.

Anyone would have said it was Gorlois.

Anyone, that is, but Merlin.

"Now," said Merlin, helping the new Gorlois onto his horse, "ride!" He slapped the horse on the flank, and it hurtled toward the castle.

Within the castle walls, Morgana, the three-year-old daughter of Gorlois and Igraine, was crying.

"My poor father is dead! My father is dead!" she sobbed.

"No, little one," Igraine crooned, "your father is not dead!" As Igraine stroked her daughter's hair, Gorlois burst through the door.

"See," smiled Igraine, "here is your father now."

"No!" Morgana cried at the man standing before her and her mother. "He is not my father! He is a bad man!" Burying her head in her mother's skirts, she wailed again, "My father is dead! My father is dead!"

Somehow, little Morgana saw something that Igraine could not. Igraine did not know who the man in front of her really was, nor did she know that the real Gorlois, her true husband, lay dead less than a mile away, killed by Uther's men.

Morgana knew, and she cried louder and more bitterly. But all Igraine felt as she sent the sobbing child out of the room was relief and happiness to see her husband alive.

The next morning, Merlin entered the castle at the head of a grim procession carrying Gorlois's body. Using all his powers and his gentle way with words, he managed to explain the events of the previous night to a tearful and distraught Igraine. Somehow he was able to calm and comfort her.

Igraine and Uther were soon married, and Uther took Gorlois's place at Tintagel. Nine months later, in the middle of the bleak British winter, Uther Pendragon's heir was born.

Gazing adoringly at her tiny new son, Igraine rocked the baby tenderly. Suddenly Merlin burst through the door, with Uther behind him.

"Merlin, I beg you to reconsider!" Uther cried.

"You swore by your kingship!" Merlin bellowed. He stormed over to Igraine and, displaying surprising strength for an old man, wrenched the baby from her arms.

"No!" Igraine screamed. "My son!" She could not understand why Merlin had suddenly changed from a kind old man into a vicious thief.

"Please, Merlin, my only son!" begged Uther, trying to stand in the old man's way. "He does not even have a name yet."

With the child still in his arms, Merlin whispered to Uther, "If only you could know what your son will mean to this country." Merlin kissed Uther on both cheeks, then spun around and left, his robes billowing out behind him.

Igraine's screams seared through Uther, his whole body wracked with guilt at the foolish promise he had made.

Later that day, far from Tintagel, Merlin was singing a lullaby to the baby. "Hush, little one," he said when he had finished. "Hush, little Arthur, true king of Britain. You're going to Wales, where you will be safe. Safe, until it is time."

Merlin brought the baby to Ector, a trusted warrior. "Guard him well," he told Ector, "for he is the one."

Uther Pendragon remained High King of Britain for several years, but the guilt of losing his son and breaking his wife's heart was too much for him. He died a shattered man, and, as far as anyone knew, without an heir.

Britain was without a leader once more.

# THE SWORD IN THE STONE

The bitter winter wind swirled around Ector and his sons as their horses trudged through the thick snow. The three were making the long journey from their home in the south of Wales to Caerleon for the king-making. The old king was dead, and now the bravest warriors of all the clans in the land were meeting to battle for the right to be Pendragon, High King of Britain.

"Father, I am frozen nearly to death!" moaned Cei, Ector's elder son. "Can we not stop and rest?"

"No!" said Ector. "We are nearly at the battlefield. Look! There are crowds of warriors in front of us!"

"I am too cold and tired to fight!" whined Cei. "I am not meant to be king, so why carry on?"

"I'll not have my son talk in that manner!" bellowed Ector. "Prepare yourself, boy. Take up your sword!"

Cei swung round to reach for his sword. Suddenly he gasped. "Father! My sword is gone!" he said.

"What?" shouted his father. "You cannot become Pendragon without a sword! How could you have been so careless?"

Ector's younger son, Arthur, a boy of only seventeen, spoke up.

"I saw a smithy a few miles back," he said. "I could hurry and fetch Cei a new sword."

Ector broke into a smile. "You see, Cei! Your younger brother has been watchful! Perhaps he would make a better Pendragon! Here is some gold," he said, turning to Arthur. "Go and buy Cei a fine new sword."

Arthur turned his horse and sped off through the snow. But to his dismay, the smithy was shut, and all the doors were barred.

Glancing around, Arthur noticed a path a few yards away. Curious, he followed it into a small grove. In the middle of the grove was a large, moss-covered stone with a sword plunged deep inside it. Nearby lay an old man with long white hair and beard, fast asleep.

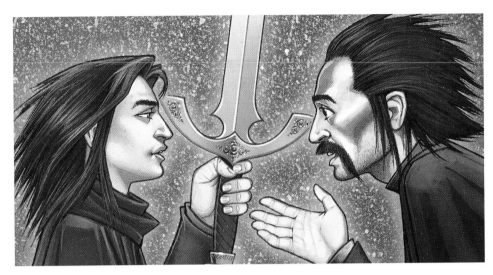

"This must be his sword," Arthur thought. "I'm sure he wouldn't mind if I just borrowed it for a while. I'll return it as soon as the battle is over."

Arthur grabbed the weapon and slid it easily from the stone. As he turned to go, he saw his brother riding towards him.

"What's taking you so long, Arthur?" Cei shouted. "The battle is about to start!"

"Sorry, Cei," Arthur stammered. "But look at the magnificent sword I have for you!"

"This is a fine weapon," said Cei, admiring the gleaming blade and the jewel-encrusted handle. "Thank you, Arthur!"

The two rode to the battlefield together. Ector was waiting uneasily, but his impatience turned to amazement when Cei showed him his new sword.

"This is Caliburn, the sword of the Pendragons!" whispered Ector. "This is the prize for the victor in today's battle! Arthur, how did you get it?"

"It was stuck in a stone," Arthur began, "and..." Before he could finish, Cei interrupted.

"...and I pulled it out, Father," said Cei. "Arthur didn't get it, I did. That must make me the Pendragon!"

Hearing Cei's shouts, some of the warriors rode over from the battlefield to see what the commotion was about.

"Show me where you found this, son," said Ector.

The crowd followed Ector and his sons to the grove near the smithy. The old man was awake now, smiling wryly at the group coming toward him.

"Where did you find the sword, Cei?" asked Ector.

Cei looked at the old man, and knew that he couldn't lie any more. "I didn't, Father," he said quietly, hanging his head. "Arthur did."

Stifling his anger, Ector turned to his other son. "Arthur," he said, "show me where you found it."

The crowd held its breath as Arthur put the sword back into the stone.

"What trickery is this?" shouted a man in the crowd. "The sword is meant to be lying on the stone, as a prize for the winner of the battle." More angry shouts joined his.

Holding up his hands for silence, the old man stepped forward.

"This sword is too great a prize for the winner of a mere battle," he said.

"You have come to choose the High King today. A different test is needed. I am Merlin the Druid, and I have put a spell on this sword. Only the one who can draw it from this stone is the true-born King of Britain!"

A great cry arose, and men began pushing forward to get to the sword. But not even the mightiest warrior could budge it. None of these men was the true Pendragon.

At last only Arthur remained.

"The boy will try now," Ector declared.

"The boy?" someone shouted scornfully. "He's not old enough to shave, much less be Pendragon!" A ripple of laughter ran through the crowd.

"He will try!" said Ector, leading Arthur up to the stone.

Arthur wrapped his hands around the jewel-encrusted handle and pulled. The sword slid from the stone like a fish cutting through the calm waters of a lake.

Instantly, the crowd fell silent.

"How can I be king?" Arthur whispered.

Merlin came forward. "Arthur," he said, "you are the son of Uther Pendragon, clan chieftain and High King of Britain. You are the true Pendragon."

"No!" cried Arthur. "Ector is my father! You are lying, old man!"

"They are not lies, Arthur," said Merlin gently. "I was advisor to your father, and to his father before him. I have been waiting for you."

"Merlin is telling the truth," said Ector, putting his arm around Arthur's trembling shoulders. "He brought you to me when you were only a baby, and told me to raise you as my own. I did not know then who you were. But it is all clear to me now."

"So you are not my father?" Arthur breathed. "Cei is not my brother?"

"I may not be your true father," replied Ector, "but I love you as my own. And because of that love I know that you must take your seat as Pendragon. You are the chosen one, Arthur, whom the Druids of old spoke of in their prophecies. Now your time has come."

Ector kissed Arthur on both cheeks, then stepped back.

"Kneel!" he shouted to the crowd. "Kneel before the Pendragon of Britain!"

Arthur gazed at the sword in his hand. The air was cold, but the sword felt warm and alive, and a surge of energy coursed through Arthur's body.

There, in the winter sun, with the melting snow under his feet, he raised Caliburn above his head. He was no longer just Arthur, a shy and quiet young boy. He was Arthur Pendragon, Chieftain and High King of Britain.

# THE SAXON WARS

Britain had a leader at last. But across the sea, her enemies were preparing for war. For years, the Saxons had been waiting to invade Britain. Now that an inexperienced young boy was on the throne, the Saxon king, Aelle, saw his chance. He gathered an army and began invading settlements along Britain's southern coast.

News of the raids reached Arthur, who quickly assembled a war council at Camelot, his fortress in northern Wales. The council was made up of the wisest and bravest chieftains in the land. As they sat at the long table in Camelot's great hall, torches crackling on the walls, a chieftain named Uriens began to laugh.

"What amuses you, Uriens?" Arthur asked.

"You are so young, Arthur," the chieftain replied, "and you know nothing of war. When your father was king, war was a way of life. I was worried at first that it would end under your rule, but now there is the promise of fighting, so my mind is at ease. War stirs the soul, Arthur, and I delight in it!"

For a moment, a biting silence hung in the air. Then Arthur shattered it by slamming his fist down on the table.

"No!" he bellowed. "No councillor of mine shall take delight in the death of others. War is a hateful thing!" He stopped, then spoke again in softer tones. "Nevertheless, if my country requires it, we must fight. We must protect our people and drive the Saxons out."

So it was agreed. Arthur prepared his army, and, on a warm, breezy morning, led his men out of Camelot.

Over the next few weeks, Arthur's army managed to crush only a few small raiding parties. Most of the Saxon army evaded their grasp, and the attacks continued. Arthur had to keep his army constantly on the move.

The war dragged on for almost a year. Arthur saw the seasons change, the trees turn, and the days lengthen as he made his own journey into manhood. War is a terrible thing, he thought, if it can turn a boy into a man in but a year.

One night, just after dark, Arthur and his most trusted aides, Cei and Bedwyr, sat around a fire in a grassy field. They talked about military tactics, and about the future and the past. Merlin played his harp and told tales of the bravery of Celtic warriors in days gone by.

Just as they were beginning to grow drowsy, a young messenger galloped up on a tired horse.

"My lord," the boy panted, "the Saxons are taking up positions near Mount Badon. Their entire army has gathered there!"

"Mount Badon?" snapped Bedwyr. "That's just half a day's march from here!"

Mount Badon was a small hill outside Bath, an important city in Roman times. If the Saxons captured the hill, they would be able to take over the city, a perfect place to bring in more men and supplies. But if Arthur and his men defeated the Saxons here, they could drive them out of Britain once and for all. It was the decisive battle they had all been waiting for.

Arthur jumped up and stamped out the fire. "Prepare the men," he told Cei and Bedwyr. "We will march at dawn."

They arrived at Mount Badon just before midday. The Saxons had already begun moving up the hill and so had the advantage of the higher ground. If Arthur charged them now, he would surely lose. The Celts had no choice but to wait for the Saxons to attack.

Arthur rode out in front of his troops. "Many of you will die today," he told them. "I cannot lie about that. What I can say is that in your dying, something far greater will be born—a peaceful, united Britain."

Merlin then said an ancient Druid's blessing over the men, and Arthur arranged the troops to form a shield wall against the Saxon charge. Some mumbled short prayers as they prepared for the attack.

Within seconds, the Saxons began rushing down the hill. Arthur wheeled his steed around and beckoned for a small group of mounted warriors to follow him. As the Saxons reached the shield wall, the Celts on horseback smashed into their flank. The shield wall broke, and the Celts charged the Saxons, scattering them instantly.

But the Saxons managed to recover and retaliate fiercely. The battle raged all day, the clever tactics and passion of Arthur's Celts winning out one minute, the aggression and force of the Saxons taking over the next.

By the time the sun was setting, it was the Celts who had the upper hand. A few stubborn Saxon warriors continued to fight, but most of them willingly surrendered.

The battle was over. The Saxons were defeated. Men lay dead all around, and the soft grass was stained red.

On the crest of Mount Badon, the Saxon king Aelle knelt at Arthur's feet, his hands bound behind his back, Cei's knife at his throat.

"Shall I do it?" Cei asked

"No," Arthur said, drawing Cei's hand away. He untied Aelle and raised him up.

"You fought well. Gather what is left of your army and go home. Do not return here again."

Arthur's aides were as shocked as Aelle, who stared deeply into Arthur's eyes. "You are a worthy opponent, Arthur Pendragon," was all he said.

Arthur Pendragon reassembled his army, raised his banner once more, and began the march back to Camelot. His knights returned to Camelot as the liberators of a nation, and leading them was not a boy, but a man—a man who was a king.

# EXCALIBUR

Although Arthur had defeated the Saxon invaders at Mount Badon, a few renegade warriors remained, and in the days following the battle Arthur and his army had several skirmishes with these small Saxon bands.

In one such fight Arthur found himself surrounded by warriors. He whirled his sword around his head like a windmill, and hacked and slashed his way through them. Just as he was stumbling out of the circle they had formed around him, one Saxon brought his sword crashing down on the blade of Arthur's weapon. The metal shattered into several pieces, leaving a useless stump in Arthur's hand.

Arthur rolled to his left to avoid another blow of the weapon, and quickly snatched a sword from a wounded soldier who lay on the ground. He continued fighting with this, and he and his men managed to defeat the Saxons.

After the battle, Arthur returned to the fields where his army had camped, and sought out Merlin.

"Merlin," Arthur said miserably, "look at what the Saxons have done to the sword of the Pendragons."

Merlin said nothing, but took the stump of Arthur's sword from him, and moved silently forward. He motioned for Arthur to mount his horse, and Merlin himself did likewise.

"Where are we going?" the young king asked.

"Follow," was Merlin's only reply. As the late afternoon sun began to sink, he led Arthur down narrow, unfamiliar paths. They rode for what seemed like hours. At last, toward dusk, Merlin alighted and told Arthur to do the same.

Merlin tied both their horses to a pointed rock and beckoned for Arthur to follow him into what looked like a dense forest. It turned out to be nothing more than a thick, circular copse on top of a sloping embankment. Below the embankment was a lake, and on its bank was a stone altar. When he saw it, Arthur knew that he was on sacred ground.

"Look towards the middle of the lake," said Merlin calmly.

Arthur looked out, mesmerized by the magical tranquillity of the surroundings. Suddenly the glassy surface of the lake began to ripple. Arthur bristled with anticipation, then gasped as an arm, clothed all in white, burst through the water. It was holding a sword, which caught the last rays of the sun and reflected them back in a spectacular, fiery display.

The sword was dazzling. Its blade shone with the radiance of the brightest star, and its jewel-encrusted handle and hilt were engraved with intricate carvings.

"Take it!" whispered Merlin. "Take the sword! It's yours."

"But how shall I get it?" whispered Arthur.

Merlin jabbed a finger towards the water's edge, where Arthur saw a small boat bobbing gently near the shore. Arthur was certain it hadn't been there when they arrived.

"What...?" he breathed.

"Get in!" ordered Merlin.

Arthur did so, and Merlin stepped in after him.

Merlin pointed his staff, and the boat began to slice its way through the water towards the arm. When they reached it, Arthur stretched out a hand and took the sword. He held it up and admired its immense beauty.

"It is your sword, Arthur," said Merlin. "It is Excalibur, forged in Avalon, the Otherworld, by the Lady of the Lake herself."

Arthur was awestruck. The Lady of the Lake—the powerful spirit who guarded the entrance to the Otherworld—had blessed him with this sword! All the way back to shore, he gazed at it, too overcome to speak, or even to read the words he saw engraved on the blade.

When they were back on land, Merlin drew a golden scabbard from within the folds of his robe and held it out to Arthur.

"This is the scabbard for your sword," he explained.

Arthur was disappointed. Next to the splendid sword, the scabbard looked plain and unimportant.

"Which do you like more," Merlin asked, "the sword or the scabbard?"

Arthur could not lie. "The sword," he replied. "I can win wars and defend my land and people with this magnificent sword. But what use is the scabbard to me, especially one so ordinary? I could easily do without it."

"Looks can be deceiving," Merlin said. "The sword will serve you well, but with this scabbard at your side, no sword, spear, nor any weapon carried by any son of earth shall harm you. Take good care of the sword, Arthur, but make certain you never lose the scabbard."

That night, before he lay down to rest, Arthur took a final look at his new sword. This time, he looked closely at the words etched on the blade.

"*Take me up,*" he read aloud. Turning the sword over, he read the words on the reverse: "*Throw me back.*"

The words were as mysterious to Arthur as everything else that had happened that day. With a yawn, he replaced the sword in the scabbard and, clutching it to him to keep it safe, he was soon fast asleep. When he awoke the next morning, he once again gazed in wonder at the beauty of this mighty sword … his sword: Excalibur.

# THE BIRTH OF A DREAM

The responsibility of being king weighed heavily on Arthur. After Mount Badon, he spent more and more time alone, thinking and worrying. He still joined his warriors for games and battle practice, but in the evenings he disappeared to dine alone in his room. Merlin tried to coax him back, saying that the men missed him. But Arthur kept to his solitary ways, joining the others only when there was a visiting chieftain. Arthur did not enjoy these formal meetings, but he knew that they were necessary to keep the tribal leaders loyal.

One of those leaders was Leodegrance, an old friend of Uther, Arthur's father. A few months after Mount Badon, Leodegrance came to feast with Arthur. He and his procession arrived early in the morning, and Arthur spent the day showing the chieftain around Camelot and introducing him to some of his warriors. Leodegrance seemed impressed.

When darkness fell, Arthur, Merlin, and Arthur's closest warriors piled into the great hall, followed by Leodegrance and his aides. But Leodegrance would not sit down.

"Where is Guinevere?" he shouted, looking toward the door. Suddenly a smile spread across his face.

"My dear!" he said, opening his arms to the young woman who was just entering.

Arthur turned to look, and what he saw took his breath away.

She is beauty itself, Arthur thought, gazing at the vision who was walking toward Leodegrance. Her flame-red hair cascaded down her back like a gentle summer rainfall, and her hazel eyes were lit by a soft, warm smile.

Arthur was enchanted. But he knew that his father had been captivated by another man's wife in just this way, so he chose his words carefully.

"Your wife is truly beautiful, Leodegrance," Arthur said.

Leodegrance roared with laughter. "Would that I had a wife so young or so beautiful!" he said. "Guinevere is my daughter!"

Arthur breathed a sigh of relief. "Forgive me," he said sheepishly.

Throughout the feast, Leodegrance chatted to Arthur, but Arthur was not really listening. He spent the whole evening gazing at Guinevere. The next morning, he went to speak to Merlin.

"You know, Merlin," he began, "I have been lonely recently. I am a king … and a king should have a queen."

Merlin sighed. "You'll have to ask Leodegrance first," he said.

Arthur grinned shyly. "How did you know?" he asked.

"The simplest of fools would know, Arthur," Merlin replied.

Later that morning, Arthur invited Leodegrance to stay for another week.

Leodegrance smiled knowingly. "Arthur," he said, "you have my permission and my blessing to court my daughter. We will stay six more days."

Arthur shook his head, realizing how obvious his wishes were. But he was pleased.

Over the next few days, Arthur and Guinevere spent a great deal of time together. They went for walks and rides, and stayed up talking late into the night. When it was time for Guinevere and her father to leave, Arthur went with them to the gate.

"Guinevere," he said, "I have felt lonely until now, bearing the burden of a kingdom on my shoulders. But when I am with you, I feel whole. Will you be my queen?"

Guinevere smiled. Over the past few days, she too had fallen in love, and she had been waiting and hoping for this moment.

"Yes," she replied.

A month later, Leodegrance and Guinevere returned to Camelot, along with loyal chieftains from across the land who had come to pay homage to the Pendragon on his wedding day.

Merlin conducted the ceremony. Once it was over, and before the festivities began, Arthur and Guinevere were led into the great hall. There, in place of the old long, narrow table, they saw a round one, majestic and gleaming in the torchlight.

"The Round Table," said Leodegrance, "is my wedding present to you and your queen, Pendragon."

As Arthur thanked Leodegrance, a vision began forming in his mind: he saw all the chieftains of all the clans of Britain gathered around one table, discussing laws and debating issues together, keeping the peace of the land. With this table as his symbol, he could unite the island.

He asked all the chieftains present to sit down at the table. Then he stood to address them.

"My lords," he said, "we have fought together against the Saxons. War creates a bond between men, and tonight we must strengthen that bond, so that it never breaks. Here, at this table, we are all equal. The Round Table has no head, nor any foot. Although we hail from different tribes and clans, at the Round Table we are all Celts of Britain, with an equal voice."

Some warriors banged their fists on the table in approval, and cries of "Hear! Hear!" echoed around the room.

"We will meet here twice in every month," Arthur continued. "As we are united around this table, so shall we be united Celts in Britain!"

The chieftains clapped and cheered. There, in the great hall of Camelot, on the night of Arthur Pendragon's wedding to Guinevere, the dream of the Round Table was born.

# GAWAIN AND THE GREEN KNIGHT

It was midwinter, and bitter cold. In the great hall of Camelot the knights of the Round Table sat wrapped in their cloaks, eagerly awaiting the meal that would soon come steaming from the great hearth in the next room.

To pass the time before the food arrived, King Arthur proposed that a tale should be told, one of bravery and great deeds. Arthur turned to Merlin, but before the old man had a chance to rise, there was a thunderous clattering at the gates, and a rider burst through the doors.

The men were taken aback. No one entered the hall of Camelot on horseback, let alone unannounced and without permission. When they took a closer look at their guest, they had an even bigger surprise.

Everything about the man—his skin, his clothes, his horse, his hair—was green. Only the whites of his eyes and his gleaming white teeth shone through the mask of green. In one hand he carried a large axe. In the other he held a sprig of mistletoe, a holy plant to the Celts, to show that he did not come in anger.

"Men of Camelot, I come in friendship," said the Green Knight, getting down from his horse and laying his axe on the floor. "To entertain you on this coldest of all nights, I present you with a challenge: I ask that one man here come forward, and, with one blow, strike off my head with this weapon."

There was a small murmur from the men, but it was quickly hushed as the Green Knight spoke again. "There is just one condition," he added. "I am to do the same to him in a year and a day."

The hall was silent. Not a single warrior wished to take up the terrifying Green Knight's challenge.

The Green Knight began to laugh—so loudly that the walls shook. "I had heard," he roared, "that the men of the Round Table were the bravest in all the land. Now I see the truth, and I am quite disappointed."

This was too much for Arthur. He could not have his loyal, courageous warriors spoken of this way. He stood up.

"I will do it, sir," he announced to the Green Knight.

But before Arthur could step forward, Gawain, a young warrior from the far north, stopped him.

"No. The Pendragon must not go," said Gawain. "I will do it." He turned to address the Green Knight. "I am Gawain. I accept your challenge."

"Gawain, you are a credit to yourself and this table," said the Green Knight. "Come and take my axe."

Gawain did so, and the Green Knight knelt and bared his neck.

"One blow, Gawain," he reminded him.

Gawain struggled to lift the heavy axe, but at last he held it over his head and took his swing. He made a clean cut through the Green Knight's neck. Instantly his head fell from his body and rolled across the floor.

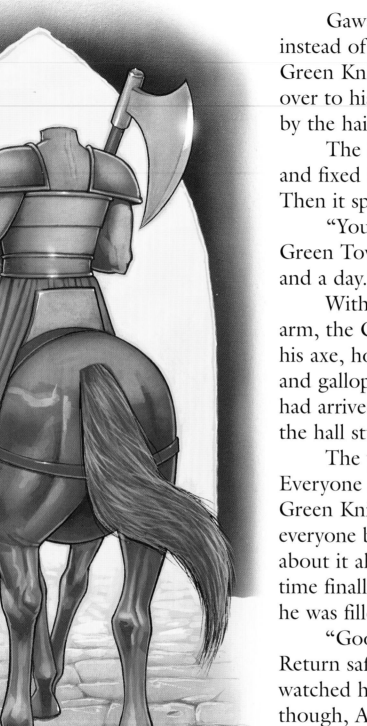

Gawain jumped back. But instead of toppling over, the Green Knight got up, walked over to his head, and picked it up by the hair.

The head cleared its throat and fixed its eyes on Gawain. Then it spoke.

"You will find me at the Green Tower," it said, "in a year and a day."

With his head under his arm, the Green Knight picked up his axe, hopped onto his horse, and galloped out as quickly as he had arrived, leaving the men in the hall stunned.

The year passed quickly. Everyone seemed to forget the Green Knight's challenge—everyone but Gawain. He worried about it all year, and when the time finally came for him to leave, he was filled with dread.

"Good luck, Gawain. Return safely," Arthur said as he watched him go. In his heart, though, Arthur did not believe he would ever see Gawain again.

Gawain rode for days
through treacherous, frozen
woodland paths. Bands of robbers
roamed the forests, and wild
beasts howled all around him.
Gawain took shelter in peasants'
cottages and woodcutters' huts,
and wherever he went he asked
the way to the Green Tower. Still,
he was never sure he was going in
the right direction.

Finally, just a few days before he was supposed to meet the Green
Knight, Gawain was close to giving up. Icy sleet lashed down from the
sky, and he felt he did not have the strength to go on. But just as he
was about to turn back to Camelot, he saw a fortress on the horizon,
and galloped toward it. When he arrived he banged hard on the gate,
and begged the gatekeeper to let him in.

The lord of the fortress came to meet Gawain in the courtyard.

"I am Bertilak," he said. "We are privileged to welcome a knight of the Round Table."

After dinner that evening, Bertilak invited Gawain to stay for a few days. When Gawain explained that he had to be at the Green Tower in four days, Bertilak exclaimed, "The Green Tower is less than a day's ride from here! Stay for another three days."

Then Bertilak suggested that they play a game over the next few days. "Anything that I acquire while you're here I'll give to you, and you must do the same for me."

The game seemed a little strange to Gawain, but he agreed.

Early the next morning, Gawain was awakened by a knock at the door. It was Bertilak's beautiful wife, who came in and sat on the bed.

"Good morning, Gawain," she said. "I have heard many tales of your bravery in the wars. Such courage deserves a reward."

She leaned toward Gawain and kissed him.

Stunned, Gawain could only murmur, "Thank you, my lady."

The lady just smiled and left.

That afternoon, when Bertilak returned from the hunt, he presented Gawain with a small fox.

"And what do you have for me?" he asked.

In reply, Gawain reached up and kissed Bertilak, who roared with laughter.

"I won't ask how you came by that!" he chuckled.

The next morning the lady visited Gawain again, and again she kissed him. Later, Bertilak again presented Gawain with the morning's catch, and again received a kiss.

"You're a lucky man to be getting all these kisses," he laughed.

On the third day, the lady came to Gawain yet again.

"You go to meet the Green Knight tomorrow. Please take this," she said, holding out a green sash. "If you wear it, nothing will harm you."

Then, as before, she kissed him and left.

When Bertilak returned, the usual exchange took place—he gave Gawain a squirrel, and Gawain gave him a kiss. But Gawain did not give Bertilak the sash, knowing that without it he would surely die.

The next morning, Gawain wrapped the sash around his waist and followed Bertilak's directions to the Green Tower. The Green Knight was waiting for him, axe in hand.

"I am pleased to see you have kept your promise," boomed the huge man. "Now, kneel."

Gawain did so, and clenched his fists, waiting for the blow. He felt the air rush across his neck as the Green Knight's axe came down. But the blade never struck him.

"What trickery is this?" he shouted.

"I am allowed one blow," the Green Knight replied. "That was not a blow."

He raised the weapon again, but again he stopped before he hit Gawain's neck. Then he raised the axe a third time and brought it down. This time it just scraped Gawain's neck. Jumping up, Gawain drew his sword.

"You have had your blow!" he cried. "Now prepare to fight!"

"Put away your sword, Gawain," the Green Knight said calmly. "You are in no danger from me."

"Why?" asked Gawain. "Who are you?"

"I am Bertilak," he replied, "the very man you have been staying with for the past three days."

"B-but…," stammered Gawain, "how can that be?"

"Morgana, half-sister of Arthur Pendragon, placed me under a spell," said Bertilak, "and turned me into the Green Knight. She sent me to test the bravery of Camelot's warriors, and so I offered my challenge—the challenge only you were bold enough to accept."

"But why did you not cut off my head?" asked Gawain.

"I missed you the first two times because you kept your promise to me and gave me the kisses I had told my wife to give you. I scratched you the third time because although you gave the kiss, you kept the sash."

Gawain looked down, ashamed. "I have been dishonest," he admitted. "I don't deserve my seat at the Round Table, and I didn't deserve your hospitality." He knelt again. "Take my head."

"Get up, Gawain," said Bertilak. "Nobody is perfect, but you have come closer than most. Go back to Camelot with pride—you are an almost perfect knight."

Everyone at Camelot was astonished when Gawain returned, alive and well. When he told his amazing tale, Arthur decreed that every year, on the anniversary of his return, everyone at the Round Table should wear a green sash to remember the deeds of Gawain, the almost perfect knight.

# LANCELOT

Just before dawn, a small ship drifted to shore on the rocky Welsh coast. A moment later, its two passengers alighted onto the wet sand, followed by their horses, prompted down the gangplank by the crew. Then, lest they be mistaken for Saxon raiders, the crew heaved the boat back into the tide and began rowing home to Brittany.

The two men who stood on the beach were dressed in simple tunics and plaid trousers. At the side of the taller of the two men hung a short sword.

"Come," he said, as they mounted their horses, "let us find the king."

Later that morning, rain splashed down on the fortress of Camelot. Inside the castle walls, Arthur and Cei were saddling their horses.

"Must we go riding?" grumbled Cei. "Look at the weather."

"It's just rain," Arthur replied. "It won't hurt us."

Cei sighed. Arthur might have been his younger foster brother, but he was also the king—and he had a mind of his own, which could not often be changed. When Arthur jumped on his horse and galloped off, Cei reluctantly followed.

In a field barely half a mile away, two riders had tied their horses to a gnarled old oak tree, and were sheltering beneath the broad branches.

Suddenly Arthur and Cei rode into the field. The men under the tree had no idea who they were, but the taller one said something to his companion. Then he mounted his horse and cantered over, blocking Arthur's way.

"Please move aside, sir," said Arthur.

"Fight me first," was the reply.

Arthur was taken aback. "Why do you seek a fight?" he asked.

"I merely seek my match," the man replied. "In all my years, I have never been beaten. I came here looking for someone worthy of my service. Perhaps King Arthur himself will ride by and accept my challenge."

Deciding not to reveal his identity yet, Arthur peered into the stranger's eyes. They fixed him with their gaze, so that although Arthur knew he should refuse, he could not say the words. Instead, he turned his horse around and prepared to charge.

"What are you doing?" roared Cei. "What if you lose?"

Arthur was asking himself the same thing—but he had no answer. He just drew his sword and galloped toward his challenger, leaning over to swing at him. The stranger deftly ducked out of the way, then spun around in the saddle and struck Arthur on the back with the hilt of his sword. Arthur was thrown to the ground, and Excalibur went flying.

As the stranger dismounted, Arthur rolled over and grabbed Excalibur. Springing to his feet, he thrust the sword at his opponent. The blow was deflected, and Arthur made another attempt. This too was parried, but Arthur would not give up. Eventually, he forced his opponent back to the tree in the middle of the field, and it looked as if he had won the fight. But as he drew his arm back for the final swing, the challenger vaulted out of the way, so that Arthur's sword was plunged into the tree trunk.

Cei spurred his horse across the field. "Arthur!" he cried, moving in front of Arthur to protect him. But the challenger was not attacking. He was staring at the two men.

"Arthur?" whispered the young man. "*King* Arthur?"

Arthur looked at the ground. "Yes," he said at last. "I am the Pendragon."

The stranger continued to stare. The man before him was a sorry sight. His face was bleeding, his hair was matted, and his clothes were caked with mud.

"I don't believe you," the stranger declared.

"Very well," said Arthur. He pulled Excalibur from the tree trunk and held it out. The man gazed at the ornately decorated handle and the carvings on the blade, then fell to his knees.

"Your Majesty," he said, clasping Arthur's hand, "I am Lancelot, son of King Ban of Brittany. The true reason I came here was to seek a place at your Round Table, a place at your right hand!"

Arthur looked down at the young man. His intuition told him that anyone with such boldness, skill, and strength was more than worthy of a place at the Round Table. But as a wise king, he knew how reckless it would be to grant a total stranger a place at the Table without first testing him.

"Come," said Arthur, beckoning the man to rise. "Return with us to Camelot, and we will talk."

Over the days that followed, Lancelot went everywhere with Arthur. He told him about his upbringing in Brittany and how, as a boy, he had begun training to become the greatest warrior the world had ever seen.

"Although I am not a native of Britain," he told Arthur, "when I heard about the Round Table, and your dream of unity, I had only one wish—to join, and become part of something truly noble."

Lancelot had been at Camelot for two weeks when word came that the fortress of one of Arthur's loyal chieftains was under siege by a band of rebel clansmen.

Lancelot begged Arthur to let him free the castle. Arthur consented, asking Bedwyr to accompany him, along with a small band of warriors.

A week later, the men returned, victorious.

"I've never seen anything like it," Bedwyr told Arthur. "As a leader, he is incredible. And he fights like one possessed. He won the battle almost single-handedly."

Arthur turned to Lancelot. "My kingdom is in your debt," he said. "How can I repay you?"

"Milord," Lancelot replied, "you know my only wish."

At the next meeting of the Round Table, when all the chieftains of Britain were gathered in Camelot's hall, a new warrior took his place among them. He was brave, noble, virtuous, and believed with his whole heart in the dream of unity.

His name was Lancelot, and he sat at the right hand of King Arthur.

# LANCELOT'S TREACHERY

Lancelot had been in Britain for about a year now, and he was never far from Arthur's side. To Arthur, he was a close and trusted friend—but Arthur's warriors and chieftains felt threatened by Lancelot. They resented him, because his virtue and loyalty pointed up their own faults and weaknesses.

Unlike most of the other chieftains and warriors at the table, Lancelot lived at Camelot. Since he was not from Britain, he had no tribe or clan of his own, and no fortress. He was close to the king all the time, and so was always the first to know Arthur's plans.

"When the Round Table began it was a symbol of unity and fairness. No one man was better than another," Cei reminded Arthur. "But you go to Lancelot before any of your other warriors. We might as well not have the meetings of the Table!"

"Don't be ridiculous, Cei," Arthur snapped. But deep down he knew that Cei was right.

Arthur decided that he needed to find somewhere for Lancelot to live, away from Camelot—and he had his own reason for this, different from that of his men.

Arthur had noticed that his queen, Guinevere, had been spending more and more time with Lancelot recently. At first, she too had disliked his arrogance, but her feelings changed as she got to know him better. When Arthur mentioned this to her, she insisted that they were just friends. But both she and Arthur knew that wasn't true. The friendship had deepened into love.

Now Arthur felt that he was trapped in a nightmare, caught between the two people he cared most about: his wife and his best friend. He didn't want to lose either of them. For the time being, finding Lancelot a place to live was all he could do.

Two weeks earlier, the chieftain of the fortress that Lancelot had freed had died. He left no son, and Arthur saw a chance to give Lancelot a home and an adopted clan. The clanspeople did not object—they still saw Lancelot as their rescuer, and were glad to welcome him as their chieftain.

But Arthur could not keep Lancelot away from Camelot all the time. He still returned for meetings of the Round Table, giving him opportunities to meet secretly with Guinevere.

One such night, after the meeting of the Round Table had ended, Guinevere and Lancelot were alone in a half-forgotten, empty room. They were deep in conversation when Lancelot suddenly fell silent. There were voices outside. Slowly, Lancelot crept toward the door, but before he reached it six men burst into the room.

"Treachery!" one screamed. "Lancelot is a traitor!"

The men were fully armed, and Lancelot had nothing but a small dagger. He ran to protect Guinevere as the men attacked. When he could no longer fend them off, he grabbed Guinevere by the hand and bolted for the door.

They sped through the fortress, the shouts of their pursuers behind them. The men caught up to the fleeing pair just in time to see them mount two horses and hurtle out of Camelot into the blackness.

The next day, after Arthur had been told what had happened, the Round Table sat for another meeting.

"What were you doing outside that room?" the king asked the six men.

"We were just passing by," one of them replied.

"You were just passing by," Arthur repeated. "You just happened to be passing a room that no one uses, and all six of you happened to be together, fully armed? You are lying! Get out!" he roared. Then he buried his face in his hands.

When he looked up, he saw that only five of the men had left. One remained, hovering above Lancelot's empty seat.

"Forgive me, milord," he said, "but, liars or not, we have nonetheless shown Lancelot—and, with respect, the queen—to be traitors. They should be dealt with as any other traitors."

Arthur looked up at the man. He had sickly pale skin and a scrawny frame. His greasy black hair flopped across his face, and his sunken, shadowed eyes made him look far older than he probably was. Arthur did not recognize him.

"Who are you?" he asked.

"My name is Mordred, sire," the young man answered. "I am the son of Morgana and Lot, lord of the Orkneys. I am your nephew."

Arthur had not known that he had a nephew, and right now he was too upset to care.

"Leave me, Mordred," he ordered.

"But he is right!" a chieftain shouted from across the table. "Lancelot has probably returned to Brittany, and he has your queen with him! This calls for war!"

Arthur could not find the words to express how deeply he did not want to wage war on Lancelot. He had seen too much bloodshed in his reign already.

It was Cei who put into words what Arthur—and everyone else at the table—was thinking.

"Brother," Cei said gently, "you have no choice."

# MORGANA AND MORDRED

In the great hall of Camelot, Mordred laughed wickedly. His laughter echoed around the empty hall, flew through the gates of Camelot, and made its way to Brittany, where King Arthur and his army were camped in a field outside Lancelot's castle.

Arthur had just received the news that Mordred had taken his throne, claiming the title of Pendragon. Arthur's nightmare was spinning out of control. If he went back to Britain he would lose both Lancelot and Guinevere forever. If he stayed here, all his work—and his hopes and dreams—would be lost along with his crown.

For an agonized day and night, Arthur stayed in his tent alone, thinking. Merlin wasn't with him—but Arthur tried to remember all the advice his wise teacher had ever given him. At last, just after sunrise, Arthur called Gawain and Bedwyr to his tent. "Take a message to Lancelot and Guinevere," he said. "Tell them to meet me at sunset, in the forest half a mile south."

Sunset came, and Arthur waited in the wooded glade. The leaves cut up the last rays of the sun, casting a lacy pattern on the forest floor. For a few minutes, Arthur forgot his problems and let himself slip into oneness with the forest.

The cracking of a twig disturbed his thoughts. He looked up and saw two figures walking toward him.

Lancelot approached Arthur first. Falling to his knees, he clasped Arthur's hand to his face.

"Forgive me," he wept.

Arthur raised him up, and Lancelot stepped aside, his eyes cast down. Guinevere, her face shining with tears, rushed forward into Arthur's arms.

"What will become of us?" she sobbed.

Gently, Arthur led her over to Lancelot.

"Mordred, my nephew, has usurped my kingdom," Arthur told them. "I would sooner die than see Britain fall into the wrong hands. I must return and fight for what I believe in, for what I have spent my life building. Go back to your castle, Lancelot, and take my queen with you." He gripped Lancelot's hand, held it tightly, then turned to leave.

"Arthur, no!" cried Guinevere, running after him. "I want to go back with you!"

"Guinevere," Arthur said, wiping a tear from her cheek, "when my country has needed me, I have always had to be a king before a husband. That is truer now than ever, though it breaks my heart. Goodbye, my love."

When Arthur was born, his mother, Igraine, already had a daughter, Morgana. Her father was Gorlois, Igraine's first husband. Morgana grew up knowing that her father had been tricked and killed by Arthur's father, Uther Pendragon. The knowledge made her angry and bitter, and by the age of fifteen she had sworn revenge upon her brother, the last remnant of Uther's foul dishonesty.

Morgana trained as a priestess in the Celtic religion, and, with time, developed powers to rival those of Merlin himself. At a young age she had married Lot, chieftain of the Orkney Isles. Within a year they had a son and named him Mordred.

As she sat by the fire, rocking her baby, Morgana crooned to him:

"Mordred, Mordred, my sweet child, you are the one. You are the one to defeat my brother, and lay to rest the evil from which he sprang."

Now Mordred was a young man. He had been well taught, both in the arts of war and the craft of magic. But he had no wish to use his powers and skills for good purposes. His mother had filled him with hatred for Arthur, and all he wanted was to destroy Arthur's dreams and ideals.

As soon as Arthur left for Brittany, Mordred began creating conflict among the clans Arthur had worked so hard to unite. He sent false messages to the chieftains, telling them that another chieftain wanted their land, or that Arthur was taking away their place at the Round Table. Soon the chieftains had turned against one another, and against Arthur. When Mordred offered them a chance of revenge by joining his growing army, they accepted eagerly.

Once he had most of the chieftains on his side, Mordred sent messengers across the sea to Cerdic, a Saxon king who had supported the invasion of Britain years earlier.

"Arthur is weakened," the messengers reported. "Mordred, the successor and next Pendragon, offers you the chance to share the rule with him if you help him end Arthur's reign."

Cerdic was delighted, and gathered his army at once.

Now Arthur had little hope. His army, though brave and experienced, was tiny. He had only a handful of troops and the few chieftains he had taken with him to Brittany. When they returned home and landed on the south coast of Britain, they received word that Mordred and Cerdic's army was already marching toward Camlann, in Cornwall.

"We can't fight them!" the chieftains told Arthur. "We're vastly outnumbered!"

"Yes, that is true," Arthur agreed. "But what if we don't fight? Then I surrender my crown, Mordred becomes Pendragon, and he'll probably have us slaughtered anyway. If we fight," Arthur went on, "then at least we have the chance to defend what we have all worked so hard to achieve. If the dream of the Round Table must die, it should die with honour."

Arthur's words stirred within his men the same courage and passion they had felt at Mount Badon. They were ready to fight and die for their country once more.

# THE FINAL BATTLE

In his tent in a field near Camlann, King Arthur warmed himself by a small fire. Excalibur lay across his lap. It was dull, and scratched and chipped from the many battles it had seen. I have spent too much of my reign at war, he thought sadly.

"My lord," said Bedwyr, interrupting his thoughts, "your only choice is to meet Mordred in battle."

Arthur sighed. "Mordred is my own flesh and blood, but I fear you are right. I must speak to the men."

Riding out to the head of his army, Arthur knew that it was outnumbered by the hordes led by Cerdic and Mordred. But Arthur had something his enemies didn't. His men believed with all their hearts in the dream of Britain, and they were willing to die for it.

"Men of Britain," Arthur shouted, "today, you are not fighting for me or even for my kingdom, but for your children's future and the future of your homeland. You are fighting for our dream. Do not let it die."

For a second or two, silence hung in the air. Then a colossal cheer rose from the men. Arthur drew Excalibur and held it aloft. "Forward!" he cried.

But even the Celts' passion could not overcome the sheer numbers of Mordred and Cerdic's army. They suffered heavy losses, and Arthur was forced to retreat.

The Saxons cheered when they saw the Celts falling back. But across the field, Arthur was rallying his troops again.

"We have but one chance," Arthur told his men. "We must make them charge us, then attack their flank with our cavalry. It worked at Mount Badon. We can only pray it will save us now."

The army formed a shield wall, and just as Arthur predicted, the Saxons charged, allowing Arthur to lead his small cavalry force into the flank of Mordred's army. The cavalry's assault sent the Saxons into confusion, leaving them open to attack by the shield wall.

Soon the Celts had cut a swathe of destruction through the enemy troops. Saxons lay dead all around, but for every Saxon that fell, six more seemed to spring up. One man grappled at Arthur's side, tearing his scabbard from his belt. Remembering Merlin's prophecy, Arthur tried to retrieve it, but it was lost in the turmoil of battle.

Despite their gains, the Celts could not take the lead. Yet they fought on. By sunset, both sides had suffered enormous losses.

Earlier, Arthur had seen Cerdic fleeing the field, but there had been no sign of Mordred. Now, on the horizon, Arthur saw his nephew's silhouetted figure, mounted on a horse.

The time has come, Arthur told himself, and rode toward him.

Mordred turned and galloped to meet him. As they collided, Arthur swung Excalibur and sent Mordred flying from his saddle. But Mordred leaped up, and pierced the flank of Arthur's horse. Arthur tumbled down, but, still holding on to his sword, he got to his feet and grabbed Mordred. Before he could deliver his final blow, Mordred thrust his spear into Arthur's stomach.

A searing pain twisted through Arthur's body. Summoning his last ounce of strength, he raised Excalibur and brought it down on Mordred's skull. Instantly, the young man fell dead.

Arthur stumbled backwards. He tried to remove the spear from his body, but the pain was too great, and he collapsed, mortally wounded.

After what seemed like an age, Arthur felt a hand on his forehead. It was Bedwyr. Arthur could see that he had been crying.

"What happened?" Arthur gasped. "What of the dream?"

"The dream is dead, my lord," replied Bedwyr.

Arthur sighed. "Take my sword," he whispered, "and ride north with it. You will find a holy grove, where the Druids used to pray, and a pool. Cast Excalibur into it."

Bedwyr found the place after only a short ride. It was a Celtic custom to throw objects into water as offerings to the gods, but Bedwyr thought of what Excalibur stood for, and could not let it go. Then he noticed the engraving on the blade.

*Take me up*, it said.

He could not cast it away.

When Bedwyr returned, Arthur asked him, "What did you see when you threw in the sword?"

"Just the wind on the water," Bedwyr answered.

"You are lying," Arthur said. "Go back and do as I have asked."

Wondering how Arthur could have known, Bedwyr went back to the pool. But he still could not let the sword go.

"I couldn't do it, my lord," he told Arthur when he returned, "not when I read the message on the blade!"

"Turn it over," Arthur told him, "and read the other side."

"*Throw me back*," Bedwyr read aloud.

"When the time is right," Arthur said, "a king will come, and Excalibur will return. The dream will be born again. Until then, you must do as your king commands you. Just this last time, old friend."

With Arthur's words ringing in his head, Bedwyr galloped back to the pool. This time he flung Excalibur in without hesitating. A white-sleeved arm rose from the water. It caught the sword and drew it under the surface.

Bedwyr sped back to tell Arthur what he had seen, but found only some flattened reeds where the king had been lying. In the distance, he saw a black barge sailing through the mist toward the sea. He knew that it was taking Arthur Pendragon, the greatest of all kings, to his final home.

# EPILOGUE

The battle at Camlann was long and bloody, and at the setting of the sun the river ran red with the blood of Arthur's army. Both sides suffered terrible losses, but in the end, Arthur's brave men could not overcome Mordred's vast forces.

Britain had lost its leader, its king, its Pendragon. It had lost a dream, too, one that it would never truly regain. Although there were to be further rebellions against the Saxons, the Celts of Britain would never again be united under the rule of one Pendragon.

*I, Merlin, advisor to King Arthur and Druid of the Celtic religion, have taken it upon myself to tell this tale to you. I ask of you but one thing: that you pass on its message, and keep the dream alive. As long as people wish to live in peace and unity with their brothers and sisters, the dream we once shared in Camelot will remain alive, and King Arthur, Pendragon and High Chieftain of Britain, will never die.*

Savannah Welcomes You...

# Contents

## SAVANNAH AREA
# Tourism Leadership Council

Welcome!

Whether this is your first visit or a long-awaited return, it is with great pleasure that I welcome you to Savannah. From coastal expanses to historic sites, the best of comfort foods and the finest of dining, Savannah is a city whose surprises unfold daily.

The book you now hold is the collective vision of The Savannah Area Tourism Leadership Council (TLC). Representing a diverse workforce nearly 20,000 strong, the TLC is dedicated to supporting those in the city's various tourism industries so that they may provide you, our guests, with an exceptional Savannah experience. Within the following pages, you will find local insight and information to help you on your Southern journey as you explore all that Savannah and Tybee Island, Georgia, have to offer. Much like the city itself, this book contains something for everyone including the best shopping spots, family fun, golf reviews, food finds and – of course – historic points and exciting tours.

We hope you will consider this your insider's guide to all things Savannah, revealing the unexpected and unforgettable side of this intriguing and beautiful city. Most importantly, we extend to you a warm and heartfelt invitation to return often creating new memories to last a lifetime.

Warm Regards,

Marti Barrow
Executive Director
Savannah Area Tourism Leadership Council

FLORENCE MARTUS
1869 — 1943
SAVANNAH'S WAVING GIRL

© Bryan Stovall, Waving Girl

| | | |
|---|---|---|
| **700 Drayton** (*p. 13*) | | |
| 912.721.5002 | 700 Drayton Street | 700drayton.com |
| **17Hundred90** (*p. 12*) | | |
| 912.236.7122 | 301 E. President Street | 17hundred90.com |
| **Andrew Low House** (*p. 24*) | | |
| 912.233.6854 | 329 Abercorn Street | andrewlowhouse.com |
| **The Art Center at City Market** (*p. 91*) | | |
| 912.232.4903 | 309/315 W. St. Julian Street (*upstairs*) | savannahcitymarket.com |
| **Aqua Star** (*p. 16*) | | |
| 912.201.2085 | 1 Resort Drive | westinsavannah.com/aquastar |
| **Battlefield Memorial Park** (*p. 73*) | | |
| 912.651.6825 | Corner of Louisville Rd. and MLK Jr. Blvd. | chsgeorgia.org |
| **Belford's Savannah Seafood and Steaks** (*p. 11*) | | |
| 912.233.2626 | 315 W. St. Julian Street | belfordssavannah.com |
| **Café Zeum** (*p. 69*) | | |
| 912.713.6049 | 207 W. York Street | telfair.org |
| **City Market** (*p. 39*) | | |
| 912.232.4903 | Jefferson at W. St. Julian St. | savannahcitymarket.com |
| **The Club at Savannah Harbor** (*p. 77*) | | |
| 912.201.2240 | 2 Resort Drive | theclubatsavannahharbor.com |
| **Davenport House Museum** (*p. 24*) | | |
| 912.236.8097 | 324 E. State Street | davenporthousemuseum.org |
| **Del Sol** (*p. 82*) | | |
| 912.236.6622 | 423 E. River Street | delsol.com |
| **Dolphin Reef** (*p. 21*) | | |
| 912.786.8400 | 1401 Strand Avenue | dolphinreef.com |
| **Fiddler's Crab House** (*p. 5*) | | |
| 912.644.7172 | 131 W. River Street | fiddlerscrabhouse.com |
| **Georgia State Railroad Museum** (*p. 73*) | | |
| 912.651.6823 | 601 W. Harris Street | chsgeorgia.org |
| **Heavenly Spa by Westin** (*p. 92*) | | |
| 912.201.2250 | 2 Resort Drive | heavenlyspasavannah.com |
| **Jepson Center for the Arts** (*p. 69*) | | |
| 912.790.8800 | 207 W. York Street | telfair.org |
| **Juliette Gordon Low Birthplace** (*p. 24*) | | |
| 912.233.4501 | 10 E. Oglethorpe Avenue | juliettegordonlowbirthplace.org |
| **The Landings** (*p. 29*) | | |
| 912.598.0500 | 1 Landings Way N. | thelandings.com |
| **The Lady & Sons** (*p. 20*) | | |
| 912.233.2600 | 102 W. Congress Street | ladyandsons.com |
| **Magnolia Spa** (*p. 93*) | | |
| 912.233.7722 | 100 General McIntosh Boulevard | csspagroup.com |
| **Moon River Brewing Company** (*p. 81*) | | |
| 912.447.0943 | 21 W. Bay Street | moonriverbrewing.com |
| **Nourish** (*p. 85*) | | |
| 912.232.3213 | 202 W. Broughton Street | nourishsavannah.com |
| **Old Fort Jackson** (*p. 73*) | | |
| 912.232.3945 | 1 Fort Jackson Road | chsgeorgia.org |
| **Old Savannah Tours** (*p. 33*) | | |
| 912.234.8128 | 250 MLK Jr. Boulevard | oldsavannahtours.com |
| **Old Town Trolley Tours** (*p. 19, 31, 63*) | | |
| 912.233.0083 | 234 MLK Jr. Boulevard | trolleytours.com/savannah |
| **Owens-Thomas House** (*p. 69*) | | |
| 912.233.9743 | 124 Abercorn Street | telfair.org |
| **The Pirates' House** (*p. 17*) | | |
| 912.233.5757 | 20 E. Broad Street | thepirateshouse.com |
| **River House Seafood** (*p. 4*) | | |
| 912.234.1900 | 125 W. River Street | riverhouseseafood.com |
| **River Street Riverboat Company** (*p. 33*) | | |
| 912.232.6404 | 9 E. River Street | savannahriverboat.com |
| **Rocks on the River** (*p. 13*) | | |
| 912.721.3800 | 102 W. Bay Street | bohemianhotelsavannah.com |
| **Ruth's Chris Steak House** (*p. 8*) | | |
| 912.721.4800 | 111 W. Bay Street | ruths-chris.com |
| **Savannah Children's Museum** (*p. 73*) | | |
| 912.651.6823 | 601 W. Harris Street | scm.chsgeorgia.org |
| **Savannah/Hilton Head International Airport** (*p. 75*) | | |
| 912.964.0514 | 400 Airways Avenue | savannahairport.com |
| **Savannah History Museum** (*p. 73*) | | |
| 912.651.6840 | 303 MLK Jr. Boulevard | chsgeorgia.org |
| **Savannah Music Festival** (*p. 53*) | | |
| 912.525.5050 | 216 E. Broughton Street | savannahmusicfestival.org |
| **Savannah Sand Gnats** (*p. 57, inside back cover*) | | |
| 912.351.9150 | 1401 E. Victory Drive | sandgnats.com |
| **The Savannah Theatre** (*p. 51*) | | |
| 912.233.7764 | 222 Bull Street | savannahtheatre.com |
| **ShopMySavannah.com** (*p. 88*) | | |
| | | shopmysavannah.com |
| **Spanky's River Street Pizza Galley & Saloon** (*p. 7*) | | |
| 912.236.3009 | 317 E. River Street | spankysriverstreet.com |
| **Telfair Academy** (*p. 69*) | | |
| 912.790.8800 | 121 Barnard Street | telfair.org |
| **Tubby's River Street** (*p. 6*) | | |
| 912.233.0770 | 115 E. River Street | tubbysriverstreet.com |
| **Tybee Tourism Council** (*p. 47*) | | |
| 877.339.9330 | 802 First Street, Tybee Island | tybeevisit.com |
| **Uncle Bubba's Oyster House** (*p. 20*) | | |
| 912.897.6101 | 104 Bryan Woods Road | unclebubbas.com |
| **Vic's on the River** (*p. 15*) | | |
| 912.721.1000 | 26 E. Bay Street | vicsontheriver.com |
| **Visit Savannah** (*p. 27*) | | |
| 1.877.SAVANNAH | 101 E. Bay Street | visitsavannah.com |

**FIDDLERS CRAB HOUSE**

RIVER STREET

131 West River Street
Barnard Street Ramp

*Waterfront Dining*

912.644.7172
FiddlersCrabHouse.com

TubbysRiverStreet.com
115 East River Street | 912.233.0770

BREAKFAST WITH A VIEW

Sapelo Shrimp & Cream Omelet

French Toast & Thick Cut Bacon

Tubby's
SEAFOOD
RIVER STREET

WELCOME
TO

Spanky's

RIVER STREET

SAVANNAH · GA

pizza galley
&
saloon

Home
of the
Original
Chicken
Finger!

317 East River Street    SpankysRiverStreet.com    912.236.3009

© The Pirates' House - Filet Mignon with a Port Rosemary Demi-Glace

# dine|savannah

# An Epicurean Extravaganza

FOOD IS ITS OWN ATTRACTION IN SAVANNAH
AND WHEN IT COMES TO FINE DINING – BRING YOUR APPETITE

*by Jesse Blanco*

With lines that extend as far as the eye can see for deep-fried wonderfulness, you may think of Savannah more for its comfort food than elegant cuisine. But for those who take their time to evaluate the entire body of culinary work in Savannah, you will undoubtedly realize there is far more in this historic city to please your palate.

There's been an ongoing effort in Savannah to highlight the area's coastal cuisine and as a result, more and more people come to Savannah to dine rather than eat. It will take some time to turn heads regionally and nationally, but fine dining in Savannah is methodically making its way from the back seat to the front. If you are reading this, you are way ahead of the curve - *lucky you* - because each of these epicurean establishments is wonderful in its own right.

Our list begins with Elizabeth on 37th. Though you won't find this restaurant in the heart of the Historic District, the five-minute cab ride is well worth the trip. Long before the area was consistently serving up world-class cuisine, Chef Elizabeth Terry was winning awards and collecting stars for her walls both literally and figuratively. Not only is the food consistently voted the area's best by such reviewers as *Zagat*, but famous 'stars' also love it here. The list of celebrities who have dined at Elizabeth's is long and includes, most recently, Ryan Seacrest and Randy Jackson of *American Idol* fame. Both stopped in for a wonderful dinner during a recent trip to Savannah. The *blackeyed pea patty* for a starter had them asking for more. Chef Elizabeth has since moved on, but the legendary antique mansion that houses this Savannah treasure doesn't miss a beat. It's as charming inside as it is when you walk up. And if you are wondering, yes, that is an herb garden out front that they use every single day.

Equally as legendary, charming and satisfying is The Olde Pink House. Probably THE most recommended place to eat in town. The Pink House, as it is known to locals, has been doing it right and doing it well for years. The home was built in the late 1700s for James Habersham, Jr. and later became a restaurant in the 1930s. Still going strong after all these years, it's a favorite because of its unique blend of charm and top-shelf cuisine. Their *crispy scored flounder with apricot shallot sauce, creamy grits & collards* is arguably the most popular dish but the menu is diverse as well, with anything from chicken to *crispy lobster tails with sweet chili Dijon* to satisfy any appetite. Planters Tavern, located in the basement, is Savannah's most cozy watering hole with a full menu available from the Pink House's kitchen. You'll thank us later.

Savannah's River Street is a popular attraction and if you want to know where to eat for fine dining the answer is simple: **Vic's on the River**. While its main entrance may not be on River Street (located on Bay Street) the views of the river from Vic's dining room are exactly what you are looking for in a quiet, charming riverfront setting. The building was completed in 1859 and even housed Union soldiers during the Civil War. The atmosphere is perfectly Savannah and the food is as well. The *jumbo crab cakes with pesto risotto and red pepper aioli* will not disappoint.

Long before the crowds began forming on Congress Street for the fried chicken and the gift shop goodies, Garibaldi Seafood was wowing them. They've been in the same spot for 30-plus years, but the kitchen staff boasts 70-plus years of experience. The attention to detail is as impeccable as the menu. Seafood is a big part of the café's cuisine but the co-stars shine just as brightly including the veal, steaks and pastas in an Art Deco atmosphere unmatched in the city.

About two blocks down from Garibaldi you will find Sapphire Grill. Sapphire is small, but cozy and beautiful. Arguably the most romantic fine-dining setting in Savannah, the menu has delivered consistently for years. Favorites include the *toasted pepper-seared tuna mignon and crispy golden rice.*

You can't mention fine dining in Savannah without our signature steak house **Ruth's Chris Steak House**. Chef Cody Buford at Ruth's mixes up their fine selection of beef with regional favorites. The appetizers include shrimp and grits made with Ruth's classic New Orleans style bar-b-que shrimp recipe. "While we take great pride in serving only USDA Prime Beef, our seafood is also very popular with guests," noted general manager, Dominic Moraco. "Because we are on the southern coast, we need to have the best seafood in Savannah as well." If you have a group, you may want to inquire about the availability of their wine cellar for a wonderful meal.

45 Bistro, located in The Marshall House, is another favorite among locals. Their *bone-in double-cut pork chop marinated in bourbon* and a popular carbonated cola beverage (hint, hint) certainly fits the bill, as do their chef specialties. Seafood, lamb, venison and duck will offer enough to satisfy any palate.

But, as a self-proclaimed foodie and Savannah local, one of my favorite stories on the fine dining scene is Local 11ten. Located at the southern end of Forsyth Park, Local is housed in an old 1950s

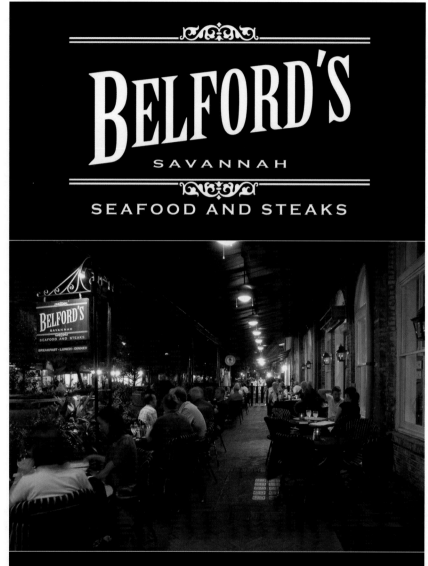

As you will discover, Savannah's options to suit your appetite are as diverse and storied as the city itself.

*Above:* Southern delicacies meet artful presentation in this dish of *chicken livers with country ham and Vidalia onion brioche over white corn sauce* from **700 Drayton**. *(see ad page 13)*

bank building. The menu is out front in what used to be the night depository. Chef Brandy Williamson learned the ropes around town in a few different spots and now is doing her own thing. On Saturday mornings until December, you may find her across the street at the Farmers Market in Forsyth Park scooping up the freshest items from local farmers to serve as specials that night. She tells me her favorite on the menu is the fried chicken ... but you won't always find it. The *Georgia alligator gumbo* or the *20-ounce cowboy rib eye* will make the carnivore in your group happy.

One of the best places to experience a view of Savannah AND have a quality fine-dining meal is at **Aqua Star** at the Westin Savannah Harbor Golf Resort and Spa. Beautiful by day and at night the soft lighting along the riverfront reminds the locals why they love this city so much. You can get lost in your own world looking back at the buildings of Factors Walk and The Cotton Exchange, which remain much like they were in the 1800s. And the views are, of course, perfectly matched by the cuisine. Looking for a specialty? How about the *Savannah Signature Pot Pie - lump crabmeat, shrimp, scallops and lobster in a Bercy sauce topped with flaky pastry and served alongside mashed potatoes and sustainable vegetables*? It is wonderful to say the least. In addition to its evening menu, Aqua Star is perhaps best known for its fine-dining champagne brunch on Sundays. Sushi to salmon, roasts and pastas, you will find it at this buffet and it is all set to the music of Savannah's legendary jazz musician Ben Tucker.

**Belford's Savannah Seafood and Steaks** in **City Market** is another signature location for fine-dining. On a cool night, patrons can sit outside listening to musicians playing in the Market's outdoor thoroughfare. Inside, the seafood, steaks and pastas are some of the most popular in town. "Our success is measured by the feedback I get from our guests," stated Kevin McPherson, partner of Belford's. "[Feedback] is what motivates me and is the best way to know what's working." Locals consider Belford's a hot spot for some of the best people watching around and there's no shortage of great food and service to go with it. Belford's jumbo lump crab cakes are the restaurant's most popular and are available as part of their famous Sunday Champagne Brunch as well. For special

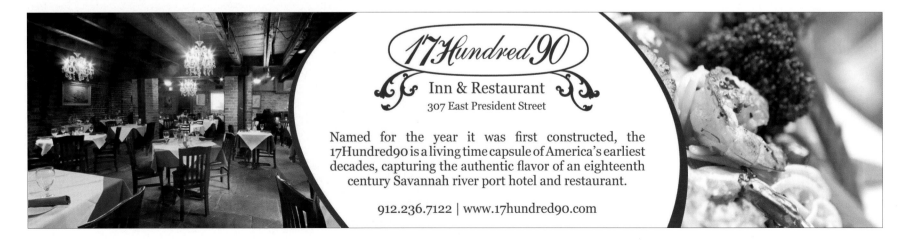

occasions, Belford's can accommodate up to 200 people and offers both buffet and seated service for groups and parties.

Then there's the trendy crowd you will find at **Rocks on the River** and Rocks on the Roof at The Bohemian Hotel. The scene is lively, the drinks are creative and the food is incredibly satisfying. I think Rocks on the River is Savannah's gourmet-comfort-food spot with meatloaf that is to die for and burgers that are among the best in town. They have also introduced a line of signature steaks, hand selected by the hotel's owner Richard Kessler.

They say you eat with your eyes first and that is definitely true of the artful experience you'll discover at **700 Drayton**. Located within The Mansion on Forsyth Park, 700 Drayton is an artistic restaurant and cocktail lounge that offers a mix of fine dining surrounded by stunning pieces of art all while still retaining the original character of this 1888 Savannah mansion. Begin your meal with a *shrimp & goat cheese polenta cake* followed by *wild mushroom risotto or pan seared Atlantic scallops* all perfectly paired with the restaurant's extensive wine list or your choice of signature cocktails. Breakfast, brunch, lunch or dinner, 700 Drayton also offers the service of private-dining specialists who can help you plan and select menus for special occasions.

While 700 Drayton may be a relative newcomer by Savannah standards, **17Hundred90** has been in service for more than 100 years. The name of this beloved restaurant and inn is reflective of the year its building was constructed and while fine dining may not have emerged here until 1966, the location's storied history makes it a top pick for colonial buffs and ghost hunters alike. "We have a varied menu and try to offer something for everyone," stated Nathan Godley, who, along with his wife, Patty and their son, Patrick, owns and operates the restaurant and inn. "We've always liked to entertain and we bring that with us to the restaurant so that our guests feel at home while enjoying our signature Southern cuisine served in an elegant dining atmosphere," Nathan adds. From decadent *crab stew* to *escargot served in puff pastry, fried green tomatoes* to the restaurant's signature dessert known simply as a *chocolate bomb*, 17Hundred90 offers guests a charming fine-dining experience of historic proportions.

For a taste of New Orleans, Alligator Soul just off of Broughton Street offers Creole-inspired selections in its exposed-brick cafe. Known for fresh, local, regional and organic fare, Alligator Soul is a romantic and elegant downtown dining establishment. And yes, as the name suggests, you can even choose an appetizer of gator and crawfish cakes to kick off your evening of Cajun cuisine perfectly.

As you will discover, Savannah's options to suit your appetite are as diverse and storied as the city itself. You will no doubt feast on fried chicken in the afternoon and dine on delectable fare the same night – thankfully, there's no need to worry about your waistline, the walking tours will take care of that – so bon appétit! ❀

# SERVED FRESH DAILY

### WHEN IT COMES TO SAVANNAH'S SEAFOOD, THOSE AREN'T MERE WORDS, THEY ARE A DELICIOUS WAY OF LIFE.

*by Heather Grant | with excerpts by Buffy Nelson*

# "An American Best City for Foodies"

*– Travel+Leisure,* September 2011

You've no doubt heard the phrase "When in Rome, do as the Romans do." And while the Romans may have never feasted on a colossal Savannah seafood platter, the good news is, you can – and should! Fresh-caught, local seafood is as much a part of Savannah as cobblestones, squares and Spanish moss. It is the official fare of locals and visitors and other than a handful of specialty restaurants, you will be hard pressed to find an establishment in town that doesn't have something seafood on the menu.

## CATCHING

In fact, seafood is so integral to Savannah life that it is a fond part of most every native's childhood. Whether going to the nearby pier or dock, or heading out for a day on the water in the family boat, all you need is a line, a net, some chicken and a little patience and soon you'll have a bucket full of the prettiest blue crabs you've ever seen.

For the truly talented among us, you can also catch fresh shrimp using a cast net. These circular contraptions are weighted on their perimeter and connected by a drawstring of sorts that the caster holds. Seeing one cast well is a beautiful site as it gracefully rotates in the air and gently falls leaving a perfect circle on the water's surface. As the net lowers the caster waits until the precise moment to snatch the rope in his hands, closing the net and bringing up dozens of the crescent-moon shaped creatures.

Of course if you don't mind getting muddy, you can also wade in the brackish shallow beds of the coast and try your hand at oyster harvesting. Whether you prefer them raw or steamed, this coastal delicacy requires some elbow grease to 'shuck' the shell open and is often served on a cracker topped with cocktail or horseradish sauce.

## CHOOSING

If you'd rather leave the catching to the pros, local fish markets are a great way to get your first glimpse of what will be on your plate at dinner tonight (and it was likely caught the very same day). That's because most restaurants partner with these markets to supply what they need for their daily fresh catch. Trey Mathews of Mathews Seafood in Savannah says they supply roughly 85% of the seafood served in local restaurants and he's proud of his family's fourth generation business saying,

*Above, bottom:* **The Pirates' House Restaurant** may be best known for its swashbuckling theme but its delicious food is also a true Savannah treasure. *(see ad page 17)*

"There's a real family feel to this business for us. We know where our seafood was caught and who caught it."

While you're browsing the market's catch or gazing at a menu, you might also notice the name *Wild Georgia Shrimp* a time or two. These wild-caught shrimp flourish in the nutrient rich marshes and estuaries of the Georgia Coast before migrating to the Atlantic Ocean. Using cone-shaped nets, generations of Georgia shrimpers "trawl" the waters seasonally bringing in an estimated five-million pounds of shrimp each year. Though the shrimping season officially runs from April through January, there are freezing processes in place that ensure their availability year-round.

And lest we forget – the fish! Grouper and flounder are found in abundance in Savannah's waters and their mild flavor and flaky white texture make them popular choices in most every restaurant. Cobia, red snapper, mahi-mahi and triggerfish are also caught in waters off the nearby coastline and served in a variety of mouthwatering ways.

### DINING

But enough about all that – let's eat! On historic River Street you have any number of delicious dining experiences that await you. **Tubby's Tank House** (with two Savannah locations, one on River Street and a second in Thunderbolt) offers diners a casual and fun experience. **Fiddler's Crab House** is a seafood-lover's dream with its fried, broiled or blackened selections. Over at **River House Seafood** their signature *Low Country shrimp & grits* keeps customers coming back again and again. For *stuffed shrimp Savannah and Caesar salad tossed tableside*, The Shrimp Factory will make your taste buds and tummy oh, so happy. Also in the downtown area, **Vic's on the Riv-**

er offers patrons a uniquely southern experience overlooking the Savannah River. In City Market, **Belford's Savannah Seafood and Steaks** offers *award-winning crab cakes,* once judged best menu item by *Southern Living Magazine.* Across the street from **City Market** at Garibaldi's, their famous *crispy scored flounder* is a dish that can only be described as sweet and salty ecstasy while over on East Broad Street the famed **Pirates' House** restaurant will delight your appetite and imagination with pirate-themed dining in a folklore-filled location.

If you are heading out to the beaches of Tybee, you'll pass **Uncle Bubba's Oyster House** on your way (owned by the brother of Paula Deen). Their *chargrilled oysters* are a one of a kind, cooked on the half shell over an open flame, then topped with melted butter and Parmesan cheese. A little closer to Tybee you'll find The Crab Shack where the 'elite eat in their bare feet' feasting on freshly prepared shrimp, fish and of course – crab. If you really just want to sample as much seafood as possible – and have a view of the ocean while you do – then the all-you-can-eat seafood buffet at **The Dolphin Reef Oceanfront Restaurant** is the perfect Tybee spot for you.

So as you sit down to your Savannah seafood feast and prepare to savor every last bite, take a moment and just imagine --- the sun rising in the east, casting its crimson glow over the Atlantic horizon with seagulls singing in chorus overhead as generations of Savannah's best fishermen set out in search of the day's fresh catch - just for you. Whether you choose to feast on crab, oysters, shrimp or fish, you'll soon discover that seafood in Savannah feeds the soul just as much as it does your appetite. ❈

© Roxify Studio

© Roxify Studio

*Above, top:* The presentation of Low Country shrimp and grits at **River House Seafood** is as stunning to behold as it is delicious to eat. *(see ad page 4) Above, bottom:* With its close proximity to the coast, Savannah restaurants know how to prepare mouth-watering seafood like this fish sandwich from **Spanky's River Street Pizza Galley and Saloon**. *(see ad page 7)*

# Y'all Hungry?

With a personality as delicious as her food,
Paula Deen knows the best way to touch your heart
is through your stomach!

*by Heather Grant*

**Is it actually possible to crave fried chicken and collard greens at 10 a.m?** It is if you're one of hundreds of visitors standing in line for the chance to savor Savannah's delicious ode to Southern cooking at The Lady and Sons restaurant.

Owner and *Food Network* celebrity chef, Paula Deen, has endeared an audience of thousands of loyal fans to her bubbly smile, mouth-watering cooking and Savannah home. And whether you say y'all or you guys, comfort-food connoisseurs agree Paula has set the bar sky high.

So how did this famous Southern lady get her start? Well in the kitchen of course, preparing lunches out of her own home that her sons, Jamie and Bobby, would then deliver to offices around town. What began as The Bag Lady in 1989 soon grew into The Lady and Sons full-service restaurant and in 1996 she opened her first downtown Savannah location. "I remember when I told my customers that I was going to be moving my restaurant downtown and I said, 'You know, y'all, that's where I belong. That's where my food belongs - in the middle of all that history,'" recalls Paula. At the time of her relocation, downtown Savannah was on the cusp of its own rebirth and thanks to visionaries like Paula Deen, Savannah has since blossomed, becoming an epicenter for culture, festivals and of course, incredible food!

By 2002, the *Food Network* realized it wasn't just Paula's fried chicken that was so irresistible and in no time a star was born. Today, Paula not only has her own TV show but a long list of highly successful cookbooks, endorsements and Paula Deen signature products for the home and kitchen. "We pretty much have products for every room of the house now," states the charming Southern cook, "from cake mixes to spices, pork products to cookware! We also designed my furniture collection including mattresses. As you can see, we've been very busy and I love it!"

Though originally from Albany, Georgia, Paula admits that hearing the childhood stories of Savannah natives does sound like fun, "They talk about growing up in Savannah and going to Savannah High and the beaches and the old movie theaters, and I'm just a teeny bit jealous!" Now that Savannah is Paula's home, she has quickly fallen in love with the city and says that Forsyth Park, Tybee Island and the Telfair Museum of Art are just a few of her favorite don't-miss attractions.

When it comes to her food's famous attraction, Paula has her own unique take on what makes her fans stand in line every day, "I think people are just fascinated with the south," says a humble but proud Paula. "I think Southern people, we really own who we are, and it comes out in the food. Our cooking has a place in history, and part of learning about a culture is eating that region's food – plus it just tastes so darn good! It's simple, it's honest, it's comforting."

Simple, honest and comforting – three words that not only describe Paula's cooking but her own irresistible personality as well. When it comes to Paula Deen, food definitely imitates life, and you can bet her devoted fans will always keep coming back for seconds. ❋

*Above, bottom:* Paula with her boys, Jamie (left) and Bobby: Television stardom and best-seller status have only brought this family closer together.
(see ad page 20)

© Chia Chong Photography

# GUIDE TO GREENS

*by Jessica Leigh Lebos*

The delicacy known as the Southern "mess o' greens" originated with the African slaves who picked wild plants and flavored them with scraps from the master's kitchen. They soon learned to cultivate their favorite varieties and have left a delectable legacy on Southern cuisine.

Dark, leafy and full of nutrition, collards are a relative of cabbage and the most popular type of greens found at the Southern table. Mustard greens—the leaves of the plant that yield the spicy yellow flower that becomes the favorite condiment on hot dogs—are also prevalent, as are kale and turnip greens.

Slightly bitter when raw, greens usually get a healthy dose of flavoring in the pot, so just because it's a plate of veggies doesn't necessarily mean it's appropriate for vegetarians: Most Southerners steep their greens with a smoked turkey leg or ham hock. Cooked slowly, they yield a tasty juice called "pot likker" savored by true connoisseurs of Southern cuisine.

Southern greens also have more purpose than satisfying the belly: There's a traditional dish called "Hoppin' John" made with black-eyed peas and served with greens that's said to bring prosperity when served on New Year's Day, and a collard leaf pressed to the forehead is considered a home remedy for a headache. But mostly, they disappear off the plate before anyone's had a chance to do anything but enjoy their taste! ✤

# what the heck are
# grits?

by Jessica Leigh Lebos

The creamy concoction known as grits starts with coarsely ground corn kernels that have been cleaned of their hull and germ—also known as "hominy"—then simmered with water or milk until thick.

Belfords Savannah Seafood and Steaks

Vic's on the River

Native Americans once cultivated maize (a form of our modern corn) in these parts, long before European colonists docked on the shores. Legend has it that they offered the settlers grits as a welcome gift.

Grits can be served for breakfast with a pat of butter and a little sugar or used to round out a hearty lunch or dinner entree as a grit cake. Grits are rarely served alone and we Southerners prefer them next to a heaping serving of scrambled eggs, smothered with sharp cheddar cheese and topped with bacon crumbles. Of course nothing pleases our palates more than the be-all-end-all dish of the Southern culinary repertoire: shrimp and grits smothered in gravy.

It's simple enough to re-create your Southern grits experience at home, just make sure you start with the old-fashioned, stone-ground kind—quick grits just aren't the same. ✿

Connecting *through* Coastal Cuisine

# One Tasty Tradition

IS IT POSSIBLE TO SAMPLE SAVANNAH'S BEST FOODS
ALL IN ONE PLACE? ABSOLUTELY.

*by Jesse Blanco*

Relatively speaking, when you are talking about Savannah, 11 years really isn't a very long time. But by today's standards, that is all the time it has taken to begin a hugely popular Savannah tradition. It was 11 years ago that the Tourism Leadership Council (TLC) held its first *Taste of Savannah®* and since then the event has grown into one of the area's premier dining events. If you want to sample delicate selections like Alligator Soul's *orange habanero smoked and braised pork with rum peach compote* or everyday fare like Leopold's silky butter pecan ice cream, you will find them at TLC's *Taste of Savannah®*.

Each year this event of epicurean proportions has a theme and in 2011, the theme was "Connecting through Coastal Cuisine." Savannah's proximity to the ocean affords us the opportunity for some of the freshest seafood you will find making the coastal theme a natural fit. A mere 15-minute drive down highway 80 out to Tybee Island and you'll see shrimp boats docked at Lazaretto Creek after a long, hard day on the water. Whether the fresh catch of the day is shrimp, fish or crab, depending on the season, you'll find the day's bounty on the table at your favorite eatery that same night … and that was also most certainly the case at this year's *Taste of Savannah®*.

The list of participants for 2011 was extensive and varied. Two-dozen restaurants lined their booths at the Savannah International Trade and Convention Center offering up their choice selections in a venue perfectly decorated to reflect an under-the-sea motif.

"So," you ask, "what about the food?"

Beginning at approximately 4 p.m. that day, long before the doors opened to the general public, three judges - accomplished Chef Jean Yves Vendeville from Savannah Technical College, Chef Chris Biscoff, an *Iron Chef* competitor, and yours truly, arrived (hungry of course) and prepared to commence with the not-so-hard work of tasting. We were informed that every seven minutes or so we'd be served a plate to sample. Time slots were assigned to the participating restaurants so they'd know exactly when their entries were going to be tasted. That guaranteed everyone a hot plate if it needed to be and a perfectly aligned presentation at the perfectly aligned time. And so we ate … and ate … and ate - Hey, someone had to do it, right?

It would be impossible to go down the line and tell you about all the wonderful dishes, which included appetizers, entrées and desserts – more than 30 in all. And as if the mere thought of this much food in one place isn't tempting enough, here are just a few of the highlights - in no particular order – from an unforgettable evening:

**Aqua Star** at the Westin Savannah Harbor Golf Resort and Spa served us a *pan seared Serrano wrapped red fish with heirloom tomato, onion and sweet basil vinaigrette on an Anson Mill grit cake*. Yes, it was that good, with the ham perfectly cooked to savor its flavor and doing a wonderful job sealing in the moisture on a delicate piece of fish. We've all had shrimp and grits (and if you haven't, you should) but a nice piece of fish with tasty ham and a grit cake was frankly something I had never tried before and it was just perfect!

Another standout was **Vic's on the River.** They offered a classic with a twist. *Peach glazed cheesecake with warm praline and peach sauce*, which took second place in the dessert category. Thinking back to it now makes my mouth water. My goodness. I've had a few pieces of cheesecake in my time, topped with strawberries, chocolate, caramel and all that good stuff, but I have never had peach on my cheesecake and I have certainly never had anything like this. For starters, the actual cheesecake was moist and creamy, as it should be. But the star of this show was the topping. Warm praline and peach sauce? If you've walked River Street a time or two, you've undoubtedly sampled the wonderful goodies at River Street Sweets or Savannah Candy Kitchen. Well, imagine that melted and drizzled on a piece of cheesecake with a hint of fruit to boot! Sign me up!

The evening's Guest Choice award for best food item and first-place winner in the entrée category came from local caterer, SAVOR … SAVANNAH: *Local grass fed beef short rib slider with stuffed Vidalia Onion soup*. This was no ordinary slider. Anyone will tell you a good sandwich begins and ends with the bread. This one was perfectly soft, fresh and sweet. I couldn't tell you if it was homemade or not, but it was perfect. As for the short rib, it was exceptionally moist and tender. I can't attest to the cooking process but I can tell you from experience in my own kitchen, this short rib was slow cooked at the perfect temperature for the perfect length of time. Melt-in-your-mouth tenderloin type of soft and delicious. The slider also had a remoulade on it, not a traditional Cajun-style sauce, this one leaned green …

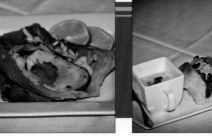

*Paul Kennedy Catering*     *SAVOR... SAVANNAH*     *Leopold's Ice Cream*

© Bryan Stovall

almost a basil-type taste to it and the marriage was divine. To top off this succulent sandwich SAVOR ... SAVANNAH served a creamy and velvety smooth *stuffed Vidalia Onion soup*, which had event guests happily tipping up their single-serving bowls with reckless abandon!

Paul Kennedy Catering's appetizer of *Caribbean pork tenderloin in romaine leaves* gave the judges a great reason to look at each other and collectively say, "Indeed, this is a notch above." The tenderloin was soft, not dry at all, sliced perfectly and placed in a fresh crisp piece of lettuce along with a mango-style salsa. It was light, it was full of flavor and it was wonderful. That earned Paul Kennedy Catering first place in the appetizer category.

Second place in the appetizer category went to StayInSavannah.com and their *Wild Georgia Shrimp and okra curry over coconut rice*. Of all the dishes that we ate and loved (and there were quite a few) this was the one that I walked away saying, "I wish I had this recipe, it is fantastic." The coconut rice was perfectly flavored and cooked. The okra curry was also a new twist on a Southern staple and proved to be a great pairing with the coconut. The shrimp? Well, the shrimp were tasty, juicy, succulent and full of flavor. This dish absolutely lived up to the billing and deserved one of the top prizes. My only regret was that I couldn't eat more. In addition to their appetizer award, StayInSavannah.com also won Guests' Choice for best booth decoration.

Finally, let's talk dessert. The *coastal pecan surprise* from Leopold's Ice Cream took home the platter award for best dessert. It was the second dessert to be brought out to the judges and I will let you in on a little secret ... I knew it was Leopold's as soon as I took a spoonful of the ice cream. As I said earlier, their butter pecan is unmatched in Savannah, all made on premises with age-old recipes, Leopold's Ice Cream just jumps out at you. To make the most delicious ice cream even better, it rested on one of the fluffiest circular pieces of pecan-flavored cake you will ever have. I don't know what was in that cake, but it was great. I am told it was the creation of general manager, Gustavo Arias. Wow. Give yourself a hand. An award well deserved.

I am quite certain work for 2012 is already underway. The staff at the Tourism Leadership Council works incredibly hard to put on a great show every single year. The themes get more lively, the spreads more inviting and, if you want to sample Savannah's best foods all at one grand event, you should definitely mark your calendars for the 12th Annual *Taste of Savannah®* on September 14, 2012. ❀

---

## 2011 Taste of Savannah® Award Winners

### *Appetizer Award Winners:*

**First Place:**
Caribbean Pork Tenderloin in Romaine Leaves from *Paul Kennedy Catering*

**Second Place:**
Wild Georgia Shrimp and Okra Curry over Coconut Rice from *StayInSavannah.com*

**Third Place:**
Regency Room Salad from *River House Seafood*

### *Entree Award Winners:*

**First Place:**
Local Grass Fed Beef Shortrib Slider with Stuffed Vidalia Onion Soup from *SAVOR ... SAVANNAH*

**Second Place:**
Braised Pork Shank from *The Olde Pink House*

**Third Place:**
Southern Style Shrimp & Grits from *The Mulberry Inn*

### *Dessert Award Winners:*

**First Place:**
Coastal Pecan Surprise from *Leopold's Ice Cream*

**Second Place:**
Peach Glazed Cheesecake with Warm Praline & Peach Sauce from *Vic's on the River*

**Third Place:**
Key Lime Ice Cream from *The Olde Pink House*

### *Best Novelty Food Item*
Sweet Potato Casserole from *Sticky Fingers Smokehouse Catering*

### *Guests' Choice Award - Best Booth Decoration*
*StayInSavannah.com*

### *Guests' Choice Award - Best Food Item*
Local Grass Fed Beef Shortrib Slider with Stuffed Vidalia Onion Soup from *SAVOR ... SAVANNAH*

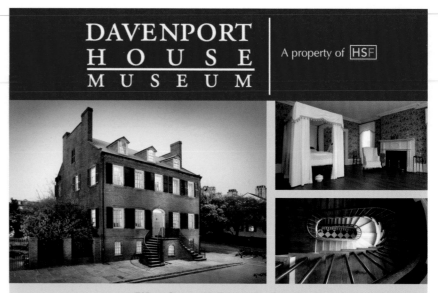
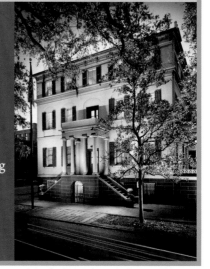

© Old Town Trolley Tours of Savannah, Inc - Trolley on River Street.

# experience|*savannah*

# Putting Down Roots

As These Sprawling Neighborhoods Prove, The Only Thing Better Than Visiting Savannah is Living Here.

*by Heather Grant*

There are those cities whose claim to fame revolves around all things "new." Still others focus solely on small-town charms. In Savannah, however, residents are able to enjoy the best of both worlds all year long. The resurgence of the Historic Downtown district has brought culture and activity to an all-time high, while organizations like The Creative Coast are attracting the best and brightest of all backgrounds and interests to the city by the hundreds. Combine Savannah's vision for the future with its preservation of the coast plus all things historic and you have quite possibly discovered the perfect spot to call home – just ask any of the city's residents.

The communities of Savannah and surrounding areas similarly offer something for everyone. From the craftsman style homes of Ardsley Park to the resort golf living of The Landings and the flourishing communities of nearby Richmond Hill and Pooler, Savannah is where those picture-perfect images from glossy brochures come to life and are lived every day.

### THE ISLANDS

If you are considering a move to Georgia's first city, you will definitely want to visit one of the first national-scale golf communities in the southeast – **The Landings**. Located on Skidaway Island, this private, gated community is less than a 20-minute drive from historic downtown but feels a world away. "The Landings was one of the first of its kind in the southeast and it continues to get better with each passing

year," commented Bill Houghton, president of The Landings Company. Home to six world-class golf courses, The Landings is an impressive residential oasis that also offers its residents 34 tennis courts, two marinas (with access to the Intracoastal Waterway), four clubhouse restaurants, 40 miles of trails and a newly renovated 48,000 square foot fitness center. The community's six 18-hole championship golf courses were designed by such masters as Fazio, Palmer, Byrd and Hills and each course is a Certified Audubon Cooperative Sanctuary. Four first-class practice facilities complete with driving ranges, chipping greens with bunkers and putting greens, as well as instructional programs offered by PGA and LPGA professionals makes The Landings a year-round golfer's paradise. With so much to offer it's no wonder that The Landings has repeatedly won *Savannah Magazine's* "Best Neighborhood" Award.

As you travel back toward Savannah's city limits, you will also pass by the quiet, tucked-away community of Isle of Hope. This quaint island features a variety of homes that truly define the quintessential neighborhood. If you find yourself touring the area, two must-see points of interest are Bluff Drive, a narrow street with expansive marsh and water views, and Wormsloe, the historic estate of Noble Jones that is best known for its highly photographed entryway canopy of live oaks and Spanish moss.

Of course it is also possible to live close to the beach and Savannah but still live in a completely distinct town. The Town of Thunderbolt can be found just off of historic Victory Drive east of Savannah and

RIVER
STREET

And *everything* in between.

Whether you crave a lively atmosphere or sweet romance.
Art galleries or song and dance. Cheddar bacon quiche
or a walk on the beach. Your Savannah is waiting.

VISIT
SAVANNAH
EST. 1733

VisitSavannah.com

LOVE
SEAT

is a unique community where families live happily for generation after generation. For those whose idea of the island life includes living minutes from the beach (or better yet, on the beach), a variety of neighborhoods on Wilmington Island, Whitemarsh Island and Tybee Island offer the perfect choice. Located approximately 25 minutes from downtown, both Wilmington and Whitemarsh Islands feature a mix of estate-home communities, such as the gated neighborhood of Long Point, as well as ranch-style homes and a variety of luxury apartments and condominiums. Just past Wilmington Island you will reach the Atlantic beach of Tybee Island where condominiums and beach cottages, along with the crashing waves, will beckon you to slip off your shoes, sink into the sand and stay awhile.

### HISTORIC DOWNTOWN

As a visitor to Savannah, you are likely drawn to the allure of the city's historic and revitalized downtown. Thanks to the efforts of those dedicated to historic preservation, the city's downtown area has become a hugely popular place to live. From older homes remodeled to look like new, to new homes designed to look old, living downtown puts you within walking distance of Savannah's culture and activity.

### MIDTOWN

Just outside of downtown Savannah, in what is considered midtown, you'll find several nostalgic neighborhoods. Perhaps the most well known of these midtown neighborhoods is Ardsley Park. Originally developed in 1909, Ardsley once attracted the most wealthy and prominent Savannahians to call the area home. Their wealth and good taste has withstood the test of time as homes with Belgian block walls and Spanish-style roofed pillars offer new owners architectural design that is as appealing today as it was when it first came to life. Another distinctive trait of Ardsley is its layout, which is reflective of General James Oglethorpe's square pattern. The neighborhood features six squares with homes that face them for a green-space view not far from the streets of downtown.

### SOUTHSIDE

As you venture south from Ardsley you will enter what is considered southside Savannah, which also offers a mix of community options including Coffee Bluff, Coffee Pointe, and Windsor Forest to name a few. Continuing further south down Abercorn Street, the lifeline of traffic through Savannah, you'll discover the community of Georgetown, which has continued to expand and grow throughout its history. Multiple smaller communities can be found within the bounds of Georgetown offering everything from single-family homes to apartments. Located just before reaching Interstate 95 on Abercorn Extension, Henderson Golf Community also offers townhome and single-family homes with access to Savannah's best and most affordable public golf as nominated by *Golf Digest* magazine.

### SUBURBS

Just outside of Savannah city proper you will find Pooler, Georgia, which is just one of a variety of choices that offer the best of suburban living in the area. Pooler features a range of home, apartment and condominium options as well as convenient access to nationally known restaurants, shopping and the **Savannah/Hilton Head International Airport.** If you're in search of a golfing community in Pooler, you'll want to consider Savannah Quarters, which offers its residents the best of relaxation, beauty and recreation in single-family homes, townhomes, home sites and estate properties. At its heart, is the exclusive Savannah Quarters Country Club, which features an 18-hole signature course designed by Greg Norman and managed by Troon Golf®. Located just minutes from downtown Savannah, residents of Savannah Quarters who become members of the Country Club can enjoy access to its 29,000 square foot Clubhouse, which incudes locker room facilities and Golf Shop, as well as multiple dining and lounging options, golf services, swim and fitness center and Har-Tru tennis courts. Future plans for this idyllic community include a center for upscale shopping and relaxing cafes.

Within the gated privacy of Savannah Quarters is the maintenance-free community of The Fairways at Savannah Quarters. The Fairways is an Epcon Community that offers residents the ease of single-level floor plans as well as access to The Fairways Clubhouse with pool, fitness facility and screened lanai. As part of the Savannah Quarters community, residents of The Fairways can also enjoy the dining, tennis courts and more at the Savannah Quarters Country Club with the option to become a member of the golf club as well.

Another suburban retreat just outside of Savannah is Richmond Hill. Originally founded by Henry Ford and home to the Ford Plantation, which not only bears his name but was also once his palatial home, Richmond Hill offers the appeal of quiet community living, coastal access and convenience to Savannah and downtown.

Garden City rounds out Savannah's suburban communities and is the second largest municipality in the state of Georgia with no property taxes. Currently, a new City Center is underway in Garden City with a vision to include walkable neighborhoods as well as new restaurants, retail shops and professional and medical offices.

While the history of Savannah is probably the initial reason for your visit, it is the hospitality you experience while here that will make you want to stay. Thankfully, the city and its communities nearby offer a magnificent choice of neighborhoods that will have you turn your vacation into a *staycation* for a Southern-style happily ever after. ❉

## Savannah's PRIVATE ISLAND CLUB *Community*

AN INTRACOASTAL WATERWAY ISLAND COMMUNITY, OWNED BY ITS RESIDENTS. Almost 40 years of national awards for golf and community excellence, with an address in one of the South's most charming and recognized cities. Amenities you would expect in a world-class destination resort, but in a residential community with the feel of a small town. It can only be THE LANDINGS ON SAVANNAH'S SKIDAWAY ISLAND.

Like Savannah, The Landings has no shortage of fun opportunities and amenities. Six golf courses by Fazio, Palmer, Byrd and Hills, four clubhouse-restaurants, two deep water marinas, 34 tennis courts, 30 miles of trails and a 48,000 sq ft fitness center - all fully owned by the members or residents – make for a great family environment. The golf and club facilities at The Landings are private, and that sense of privacy is furthered by the community's location on 6,500 acre Skidaway Island, which the gated community shares with a state park and the Skidaway Institute of Oceanography.

The Landings repeatedly wins "best community" and neighborhood awards from local publications like *Savannah* magazine, and was just the second community ever awarded the Urban Land Institute's coveted Award of Excellence. If you love Savannah, and you love world-class resort style communities, The Landings on Savannah's Skidaway Island offers the best of both worlds.

MARKETED BY
**The Landings Company**

THE LANDINGS DISCOVERY CENTER
1 Landings Way North, Savannah GA
*(about 15 minutes from historic downtown)*
Open seven days a week
912-598-0500 | www.TheLandings.com

# SEEING THE SIGHTS

## STEP BY STEP AND MILE BY MILE, SAVANNAH'S TOURS BRING HISTORY TO LIFE

*by Christine Lucas*

Introducing yourself to Savannah, Georgia, means coming face to face with a Southern lady of many layers. If you wish to hear her secrets, you're in luck thanks to the finesse of Savannah's many tour companies.

As a city, we embrace overgrown live oaks, azaleas and camellias. We delight in vines, which tickle our elbows as we pass hidden gardens. That's right; not all of our posies are fit for public consumption. To get a peek, y'all must come for the annual Tour of Homes and Gardens, which happens every spring. The **Historic Savannah Foundation** partners with Women of Christ Church, as well as corporate sponsors, to create a self-guided tour through the landmark Historic District. The private homes and courtyard gardens are vital parts of an authentic Savannah experience. Tickets can be purchased online at *savannahtourofhomes.org* starting in the December prior to the tour or in-person.

Savannah offers an astounding number of tours to suit every taste. It makes no difference whether you're here for the juice on *Midnight*, the buttery goodness of Paula Deen, or detailed accounts of the various historic events that have occurred in the Hostess City. We cater to visitors who wish to walk among our spirits and those who simply want to drink them.

John Duncan is a retired Armstrong Atlantic State University History professor who was once responsible for making sure Savannah's tour guides were up to snuff. They must pass a vigorous test in order to be licensed by the city, and he says the 110 pages created by AASU's Dr. Barbara Fertig have come even further than the manual in which he took part. "It's kind of heavy duty," he says, but also reminds visitors, "It's not the tour company; it's the tour guide." According to John, anybody can talk about a city, but passionate tour guides enjoy sharing what they've learned. It doesn't get old for them, because they get a kick out of Savannah being new to visitors! Back when John, the co-owner of V&J Duncan (a Taylor Street shop for antique maps, books, and prints), taught his 10-week course to Savannah's aspiring tour guides, most of his students were locals. Now, he admits, many have come from elsewhere and taken tour guide positions after falling in love with the city.

Whether this is your first Savannah visit or one of many, a trolley tour is essential because it gives you a broad and relaxing overview of the Historic District. The nostalgia of these vintage vehicles will instantly take you back to a simpler time, setting the perfect tone for any tour. "Trollies in Savannah are the attraction that takes you to the attractions," said Charlie Brazil, general manager of **Old Town Trolley Tours**, which transports more than 300,000 passengers each year. With an experience best described as *Transportainment*™, a term coined by Old Town Trolley Tours, passengers young and old enjoy open-air transportation while being highly entertained by expert conductors. "Trolley conductors are the ambassadors of the city," added Charlie, "they are the front-line concierge service ready to answer a range of questions from historic points of interest to the best places to eat." Savannah's three trolley tour companies each offer a range of tour routes and themes. Whether you choose the historic or haunted variety, you will enjoy the convenience of on/off service designed to ensure you get the most out of your Savannah tour. So how do you know who's who? We encourage you to visit the very informative websites of each of the tour companies, some of which offer

land and sea tours, all led by seasoned guides. Once you've chosen your tour, the easiest way to spot your selected trolley from the street is by color. Old Town Trolley Tours are the orange and green fleet and offer tours in Savannah as well as other popular tourist destinations. Currently one-third of the Old Town Trolley Tours fleet uses propane as its green fuel choice with plans to convert fully to propane next year. **Old Savannah Tours** operate white trolleys and have been in Savannah for more than 30 years. Their Historic Overview Tour covers 275 years of history in just 90 minutes! "Our main goal is to cater to a diverse range of interests and with ten different tours there is something for everyone," said Will Green, owner of Old Savannah Tours. Oglethorpe Trolley Tours are recognized for their blue trollies and if you're a fan of travel TV, you may have seen their blue fleet featured on the *Travel Channel*. Whatever company you choose, each offers something unique. Just keep in mind the color of the trolley from which you depart. While each is warm and welcoming, their tickets are not interchangeable.

There are all sorts of vehicles that will take you on tours through Savannah, but to truly explore inside the city's famed 22 historic squares you may want to consider a guided walk. The construct of General James Oglethorpe, Savannah's squares have brought military and social benefits to the city since their completion. Locals find the parks' benches beat the heck out of a drive-thru line at lunchtime, and there is no better place to gain perspective with a cocktail.

When choosing your tour, sometimes you want the excitement of a group, other times you may prefer a custom tour and if the latter suits you best, then Dottie Barrett of Historic Savannah Tours is your guide. Specializing in private, custom tours of Historic Savannah, Dottie is a licensed professional tour guide whose passion for Savannah's history, lore and natural beauty are absolutely infectious. Tour companies often call on Dottie to work with them as a result of her 30+ years of tour experience in the city. She is also routinely chosen to welcome celebrities and visiting royalty earning her the acclaim of being Savannah's number-one history tour guide.

For a slightly different approach, Savannah Dan of Savannah Dan Walking Tours will give you the Southern Gentleman's take on things. He only does one tour a day, but the limited spots allow for an intimate experience where even your dog is welcome. "I think that people are surprised history is as entertaining and funny as I make it," Dan says. He agrees that our squares will make your visit. "If you don't walk in a square and feel that 10 percent drop in temperature [a plus in our sultry summers], you missed Savannah."

If you're the sort with exploding travel journals chock-full of interesting tidbits discovered on various jaunts, then you will appreciate tours by The Savannah Walks. Brad Spinks, the owner and general manager, strives to make sure the time and energy his guests put into a walking tour is matched by its content. "We're looking for the people who are out there to know more," he says. They have seven tours a day and are confident enough to offer 100-percent refunds to unsatisfied customers. There are tours revolving around the Civil War, Homes, Ghosts, *The Book*, gardens and a new one focusing on pubs.

At night, if you see someone float through Savannah, it just might be a ghost. During the day, however, you can be sure it is someone enjoying a tour from Segway of Savannah. Located on Liberty Street, in the Drayton Tower, Harry Green and his wife, Lynn, invite their guests to see how easy it is to operate a Segway like a pro. In doing so, you will be free to see the city's architectural features up close while still enjoying a welcomed breeze.

Tours are limited to what they can fit in to their time allotment. "We're getting five or six miles on a full tour," says Tess Scheer, Director of Tourism for Segway of Savannah. Segways can maneuver well and travel up to 12 miles per hour. According to Tess, on foot, people tend to stroll and therefore can't cover as much territory. "They're not going to get in that much, 'cause they're not as mobile as we are." Tess also likes to point out the expanded field of view Segways offer. With the Segway there is no fighting other visitors for a good look, and you can see clear up to the rooftops without the interference of a vehicle's canopy. The minimum age for a Segway Tour is 15. You can also choose between a one- or two-hour tour.

## "Top 10 Culture and Sightseeing Destinations in the U.S."
— *TripAdvisor.com*, April 2010

## "Top 10 U.S. Cities"
— *Condé Nast Traveler Magazine*, November 2010

## "Top 15 Coolest North American Cities"
— *MSN.com*, September 2011

Background noises of Savannah include the splash of fountains, live music, birds, and the clip-clop of carriage horses. The romance of a horse-drawn carriage is not new, and that is precisely what makes them effective. Historic Savannah Carriage Tours runs tours seven days a week. Make reservations, because these 45-50 minute rides are in hot demand. They are not just for lovers either. Larger carriages allow families and friends to enjoy the city together. Plantation Carriage Company offers tours that are 50-60 minutes complete with drivers and ticket sellers who are in period clothing.

Finally, Savannah is a city of folks that love time on the water. **River Street Riverboat Company** offers cruises for all ages. "The view of Savannah from the river is totally different than any other view – especially at sunset," says owner Jonathan Claughton. The River Queen and Georgia Queen sail rain or shine, and accommodate those seeking romance, a good meal, or just plain fun. Savannah is, after all, a port city, and this is a great way to see the big ships that enter our harbor up close.

Every tour is different, so enjoying a variety allows you to piece together your preferred mix of fact and fun. Also keep in mind the seasonal changes to our wonderful city. March highlights the azalea blooms, while in the autumn you'll be spooked by the city built over its dead, and, at Christmas, there is nothing like the red ribbons draped around our gorgeous homes. Let there be no doubt, Savannah is a seductive city that knows how to show just enough to leave you wanting more. ✻

© Savannah Mobility Management, Inc.; Dottie the River Street Streetcar and The Express Shuttle

# Go Your Own Way

VENTURE THROUGH SAVANNAH'S HISTORY AND STREETS WITH ONE OF THE CITY'S MANY MEANS OF TRANSPORTATION.

*by Heather Grant*

You have arrived! As a visitor to Savannah, seeing the sights and hearing the stories is an essential part of your trip. While the city offers any number of organized tours, from trolley rides to horse-drawn carriages and beyond, it's also easy to find your own way via shuttles, streetcars, ferries and even bikes and segways.

## THE *dot*

As you make your way around the city, you may see the big plum-colored *dot* on vehicles from time to time. Whenever you see the *dot*, that's your cue to downtown Savannah's fare-free transportation system. The *dot* system includes the Express Shuttle, the Savannah Belles Ferry and *dottie*, the River Street Streetcar, all of which are ADA accessible. The climate-controlled Express Shuttle loops through Savannah's Historic District connecting Savannah's visitor centers, parking facilities, attractions, shops, restaurants and accommodations. The Express Shuttle operates seven days a week* from 11 a.m. to 9 p.m. providing service to 11 *dot* Express Shuttle stops. The Savannah Belles Ferry transports passengers between River Street and Hutchinson Island, where the Savannah International Trade and Convention Center and Westin Savannah Harbor Golf Resort & Spa are located. With one landing on Hutchinson Island and two on River Street, the Savannah Belles Ferry provides the perfect river respite for all onboard and operates from 7 a.m. to midnight, seven days a week.* For a more nostalgic trip on land, consider the refurbished 1930s River Street Streetcar, *dottie*, which makes stops at its six drop-off/pick-up points along River Street. Traversing the cobblestones is a breeze in the Streetcar, which also happens to be the first biodiesel fueled hybrid streetcar in North America! You can experience *dottie* Thursday through Sunday from 12 noon to 9 p.m.*

*The *dot* does not operate on certain holidays so you may want to check out connectonthedot.com for helpful information, including a map that pinpoints all stops in the city.

## BIKE TRANSPORTATION

For the avid cycler, and even the casual one, Savannah offers many scenic opportunities for you to pedal your way through. In fact, you can access four different bike-path maps by visiting *savannahga.gov* and clicking the featured link *mobility and parking services* to get all the details. Even if you didn't bring your own two-wheeled friend with you, the folks at the Bicycle Link on MLK Jr. Boulevard and Sekka Bicylcles with its two downtown locations, one on Broughton and another on Bull Street, as well as Perry Rubber Bike Shop also on Bull Street, have convenient rental options for you to see the city in cycling style. Of course, if you're up for a bicycle built for 16 – yes, 16 – then Savannah Slow Ride is just your speed. This eco-friendly tour meanders through the city streets at a leisurely 5 miles per hour and welcomes riders to bring along snacks and even adult beverages (in compliance with the city's current open container laws). Part organized tour, part freewheeling fun, you can take your pick from Antique Store Rides to Happy Hour Rides, Coffee Shop Stop Rides and Museum Rides. The more folks you have on the bike at once, the less peddling each individual will have to do so you might want to book this one in advance.

## SEGWAYS, MOPEDS AND PEDICABS

The new way to get around Savannah is the Segway. These two-wheeled stand-up marvels of modern-day transportation use your body's own forward and back movement to speed up or slow down your Segway as you choose. No experience is necessary and you can choose from organized Segway tours or rent your own for the day from Segway of Savannah. If you still want to go motorized but prefer the sit-down version instead, Vespa Savannah offers a variety of mopeds available for your renting whimsy. For those of you who want to answer the call of the open air but don't want to do the driving, Savannah Pedicab is perfect for you. These three-wheeled buggies tote two at a time and offer an experience that is part bike, part rickshaw and all fun! You can flag one down while walking around or call to reserve one in advance for a special occasion.

## MOTORIZED VEHICLES

Whether you drove to Savannah or rented a car when you arrived, having your own vehicle gives you the option to drive around the city at your own pace. The City of Savannah operates more than 3,000-metered parking spaces, five public parking garages and six surface lots. As a visitor, you are eligible for a Visitor DAYPASS, which allows unlimited parking in any city parking garage or lot as well as at any parking meter with a time limit of one hour or more. The pass is good for 48 hours from the time of purchase at a cost of $12 for two days or $7 for a single day. If you prefer the pay-as-you-go mode of parking, it's important to note that you only pay meters in Savannah between the hours of 7:30 a.m. and 5 p.m. Monday through Friday; outside of those times (which includes weekends and major holidays), no tickets are given (as long as you are legally parked that is) -- so you can save your pocket change!

Of course another very popular mode of motorized vehicle you will no doubt see around the city is the nostalgic trolley. With its open-air ambiance (and drop sides should it rain) the multiple trolley tours offered in Savannah give visitors a wonderful opportunity to see the city and hear about its history from seasoned tour guides all while leaving the driving up to someone else. There are three well-known and well-traveled tours in Savannah and they include **Old Town Trolley Tours** (*this fleet is known by its bright orange and green hues*), **Old Savannah Tours** (*look for their signature white trolley*) and Oglethorpe Tours (*with its blue and gold body paint*). You can make reservations in advance or contact their management offices once you arrive to find out tour times and availability.

Whatever mode of transportation you choose, you're sure to experience the beautiful sights, unforgettable accents and Southern charm that can only be Savannah. So what do you say – let's go! ❁

Whatever mode of transportation you choose, **you're sure to experience the beautiful sights, unforgettable accents and Southern charm that can only be Savannah.** So what do you say – let's go!

*Above, top:* Grab a slice of pizza at Vinnie Van Go-Go's, situated on one of the busiest corners in town at **City Market**. *(see ad page 39)* *Above, bottom:* Whether it's from the driver's seat of an **Old Savannah Tours** trolley or while pedaling a three-wheeled pedicab, Savannah's many tour guides each have a unique take on 300 years of history. *(see ad page 33)*

# CITY MARKET

## WHERE CITY ACTIVITY MEETS LOCAL CREATIVITY

THE WORDS ROMANTIC, HISTORIC, SERENE AND EXCITING IMMEDIATELY COME TO MIND AS YOU STROLL THROUGH THE HISTORIC CORRIDOR THAT IS AT THE HEART OF CITY MARKET.

*by Heather Grant*

Within this unique marketplace there is always something new to encounter, something different to find and something hidden to uncover. You may have to look around a corner, behind a door or up a remote staircase but that's part of the charm that makes **City Market** so special.

Since the early 1700s, City Market has been the commercial and social center of historic Savannah. Located on the original site of the market used by farmers and traders of all kinds to sell their goods and wares, City Market offers the best of what is old and new in Savannah.

Today, Savannah's City Market comprises a four-block area of restored warehouses and shop fronts adjacent to Ellis Square. This charming, open-air marketplace houses a wealth of things to do, whether you come for the entertainment, to shop, dine or just relax a moment and rest your weary feet.

Savannah boasts a vibrant art scene and City Market is at the center of it all. As you visit City Market, allow plenty of time to enjoy the wide variety of art galleries – from fine art to contemporary art – by more than 50 local artists. An especially unique experience offered at City Market is the Art Center, where you can watch artists create original works in their studios.

City Market is also home to some of the best places to eat in Savannah. Diners can satisfy their appetites at one of the many restaurants, cafes or specialty food shops located within steps of one another. The wide variety of choices will appeal to all tastes and pocketbooks with a casual atmosphere and outdoor dining that are available just about year 'round. If a sit-down meal isn't

on the menu, you can still sample City Market's best by simply enjoying an ice cream, espresso or cocktail in the public courtyard while also catching up on your people watching.

The mercantile and produce offerings of yesteryear in City Market have been replaced by an eclectic blend of art galleries and specialty shops. Shoppers will discover unique gifts, original works of art, freshly made candy and a host of other delights at the many shops and boutiques that welcome visitors to browse and buy.

Entertainment in Savannah abounds and City Market is certainly a hub for fun things to do. Outdoor entertainment, including street musicians, live music and special events, is featured in the pedestrian-only courtyards of City Market almost daily throughout the year. Indoor entertainment is also provided year 'round by many of the restaurants and bars throughout the market. As the evening nears, City Market's tucked-away nightspots offer a variety of enticing cocktails to cap off a spirited night on the town. Whether on the rooftop or on the lower level of the courtyard, you're sure to find a place that suits your preference. Additionally, carriage and trolley tours leave and return to City Market each day making it the perfect embarkation point to explore more of our beautiful city.

Depending on when you visit Savannah, you can also take your pick from a host of special events that take place in the City Market courtyards at various times throughout the year. The holiday season in City Market brings with it two very special events: The Annual Holiday Open House and Christmas for Kids Event. Extended business hours, complimentary holiday

*Above, top:* In the early 1700s, **City Market** is where farmers and traders sold their goods and wares. *Above, bottom:* The passing of time and the damage of fires have caused the face of **City Market** to change through the years. *(see ad page 39)*

**This charming, open-air marketplace houses a wealth of things to do,** whether you come for the entertainment, to shop, dine or just relax a moment and rest your weary feet.

© Bryan Stovall

© Bryan Stovall

*Above, left:* The ambiance of **City Market** welcomes visitors around the clock. *Above, right:* Shops and cafés in **City Market** often keep their doors open as a welcoming gesture to all who visit. *Below:* When you see this sign you know you have arrived at this historic mecca of shopping and dining. *(see ad page 39)*

Without a doubt, City Market offers visitors a one-of-a-kind experience in a one-of-a-kind place where **past and present beautifully combine to create a truly local must-see Savannah attraction.**

© Bryan Stovall

treats, carolers, Father Christmas and a shimmering display of luminaria in the courtyards are just a few of the highlights of this festive time of year. For the young - and young at heart - Christmas for Kids provides special family activities including decorating cookies, making ornaments and enjoying other family friendly activities and performances. In addition to the holidays, City Market also plays host to other popular annual events including the Valentine's Day Renewal of Vows Ceremony, St. Patrick's Day Festival and an Annual New Year's Eve Celebration.

Though the farmers and merchants from centuries past may have never envisioned the City Market of today, it is their entrepreneurial spirit that has enlivened this unique place into the epicenter of activity that it has become. Without a doubt, City Market offers visitors a one-of-a-kind experience in a one-of-a-kind place where past and present beautifully combine to create a truly local must-see Savannah attraction. ❀

# ❁ CITY MARKET ❁

## Art Galleries

| | | |
|---|---|---|
| A.T. Hun Gallery | 302 W. St. Julian Street | 912.233.2060 |
| Jim Pennington Fine Art | 307 W. St. Julian Street | 985.789.5547 |
| Raffine Galerie | 306 W. Congress Street | 912.232.6400 |
| Signature Gallery | 303 W. St. Julian Street | 912.233.3082 |
| Stephen Kasun Gallery | 305-A W. Bryan Street | 407.474.0411 |
| The Gallery | 20 Jefferson Street | 912.231.2025 |
| Thomas Kinkade Gallery | 211 W. St. Julian Street | 912.447.4660 |

## Dining

| | | |
|---|---|---|
| Belford's Savannah | 315 W. St. Julian Street | 912.233.2626 |
| Cafe at City Market | 224 W. St. Julian Street | 912.236.7133 |
| Cafe GelatOhhh! | 202 W. St. Julian Street | 912.234.2344 |
| Ice Cream Etcetera | 19 Jefferson Street | 912.239.9444 |
| Tapas By Anna | 314 W. St. Julian Street | 912.236.2066 |
| Vinnie Van Go-Go's | 317 W. Bryan Street | 912.233.6394 |
| Wild Wing Cafe | 27 Barnard Street | 912.790.9464 |

## Shopping

| | | |
|---|---|---|
| All Things Georgia | 305 W. St. Julian Street | 912.233.7017 |
| Cinnamon Bear | 309 W. St. Julian Street | 912.232.2888 |
| Meinhardt Winery | 306 W. St. Julian Street | 912.644.7200 |
| Mighty Eighth Air Force Museum Exhibit and Gift Shop | 204 W. St. Julian Street | 912.748.8888 |
| Nature's Treasures | 213 W. St. Julian Street | 912.234.1238 |
| Savannah Cigars | 308 W. Congress Street | 912.233.2643 |
| Savannah Prose & Poetry | 309 W. St. Julian Street | 912.232.3134 |
| Savannah's Candy Kitchen | 318 W. St. Julian Street | 912.201.9501 |
| Scents of Savannah | 33 Jefferson Street | 912.447.1817 |
| Silver Silk and Beads | 310 W. St. Julian Street | 912.236.2890 |
| Trolley Stop Gifts | 217 W. St. Julian Street | 912.233.5604 |
| Twinkle | 307 W. Bryan Street | 912.234.1001 |

## Entertainment

| | | |
|---|---|---|
| Pour Larry's | 206 W. St. Julian Street *(lower level)* | 912.232.5778 |
| The Bar Bar | 219 W. St. Julian Street *(lower level)* | 912.231.1910 |
| The Roof Top Tavern | 309 W. St. Julian Street *(upper level)* | 912.660.0033 |

# At the Water's Edge

THE SAME RIVER THAT ONCE WELCOMED OGLETHORPE STILL BECKONS VISITORS WITH ENDLESS POSSIBILITIES. *by Christine Lucas*

Savannah's River Street offers nothing if not a sharp contrast of old and new. Feel the coolness as you brush against bricks belonging to 19th century cotton warehouses. Navigate the cobblestones that have been polished by centuries of foot traffic. Let the flowing water of the Savannah River lull you into a nostalgic haze, and then watch as the sights and sounds of a modern port city stir you awake. Music and the smell of Southern delicacies escape the doors of River Street's restaurants and pubs. Confections, souvenirs, and local artwork seduce your senses further. Oh, and, hey, check out that container ship eclipsing the sky!

If you are drawn to the endless array of activities offered along River Street, you'll want to be sure to reserve your room at one of the hotels overlooking it. Your bird's eye view will help you choose where to visit first once you're on street level.

Of course one of the main attractions of any destination is where to eat. There are many great restaurants on River Street, so it is important to start enjoying them early. Huey's on the River, located at 115 East River Street, has the flavors of the South, more specifically New Orleans. "We have

© Bryan Stovall, Savannah's River Street

"Savannah's River Street: **America's Coolest River Walks**" - *Travel + Leisure Magazine*, September 2010

a killer breakfast," says daytime manager Joseph Cunningham. "That's what people come for," he adds. Their beignets are made to order and come beneath an avalanche of powdered sugar. As if that isn't enough, they add a side of hot praline sauce. It's rich enough for the most die-hard sweet tooth, but to stop there would mean missing their egg Sardou or, maybe, their award-winning bloody mary, which includes Absolut Peppar. Then again, if a heaping helping of delicious French toast sounds more your speed, then be sure to visit **Tubby's Tank House** where the balcony views are the perfect pairing to a satisfying breakfast menu full of early morning favorites.

Next you'll want to walk off such decadence and the River Street Market Place is an excellent place to start. Here you can explore two covered shopping areas filled with vendors of all sorts. Souvenirs abound and there are even cool-water misters toward the back where one can cool down in hot weather.

Speaking of hot weather, before you spend too much time in the sun, be sure to stop by **Del Sol** on River Street where every item in the store changes color in sunlight! From fun kids' wear to styles

*Above:* Factors Walk, also known as Factors Row, is a unique grouping of red brick structures that were once home to the original Cotton Exchange where cotton brokers set prices worldwide.

and accessories for adults (even nail polish!), Del Sol gives a whole new meaning to fun in the sun and will definitely be a hot topic of conversation throughout your outdoor tours.

In addition to its shops and restaurants, River Street also offers visitors a chance to remember the fallen heroes of World War II with a recently unveiled monument titled "A World Apart." The striking pass-through design of the globe-shaped monument features a granite wall engraved with the names of local service men and women who lost their lives in the historic battle. Even among the bustle and activity of River Street, the monument beckons all who pass by to pause for a moment of silence in tribute to those remembered there.

The artistry of this impressive monument serves as a beautiful complement to the many original creations showcased in River Street's galleries and shops. Gallery 209 is an artist co-op, and it is located in the Factor's Walk section of River Street. The cotton warehouse turned gallery has two floors of display area. Visitors include those seeking investment pieces as well as smaller, more affordable, pieces done by talented local artists. Beyond the Hyatt, on the west end of River Street, you'll find The Village Craftsman another artist co-op. Photographer Harold Reeves has been part of it for around three years. He's a retired biology teacher who fell hard for digital photography when his son bought him a camera. "I do landscapes and scenes of the Low Country," he says. "It's just how I see things." The 18 artisans in the co-op live within 40 or 50 miles of the shop and work in various mediums. Many will gladly ship their work. Both of these galleries have existed for decades and offer tourists a chance to embrace Savannah's creative side.

The Savannah Riverfront, a local non-profit association, is responsible for coordinating special events throughout the year with great attention to detail. Its pride and joy this year will be the *Tall Ships Challenge 2012, Atlantic Coast.* Their joint effort with **Visit Savannah** will bring quite a spectacle to the Hostess City. For three days, there will be approximately 15 tall ships docked in Savannah on both sides of the river and will undoubtedly be a sight to see.

During the Saint Patrick's Day festival on River Street everyone is Irish. It would be a mistake, however, to think we don't put on a show of some sort every day of the year. Whether you're watching large container ships gingerly make their way through our narrow waterway, or the fast little legs of dachshunds entered in our annual Weiner Dog Race during Oktoberfest, River Street festivals deliver.

You will be delighted to know that the fast pace of River Street does not diminish your chances of enjoying "slow food" prepared by excellent and experienced chefs. Located on Lincoln Street, between West Bay and River Street, you'll find the Boar's Head Grill & Tavern where local owners Philip and Charlene Branan will treat you right. Philip is also the Boar's Head Tavern's skilled chef and he and his staff definitely prove that a tourist location doesn't mean sacrificing quality. "We do everything from scratch," Chef Philip says.

© Visit Savannah

© Old Town Trolley Tours of Savannah, Inc.

*Left:* Shopping along the Savannah River Front is an unforgettable experience. *Right:* It is easy to get lost in River Street's towering tribute to history, just don't look up too much, those cobblestones can be tricky!

**River House Seafood**, located at 125 West River Street, has the charm you'd expect and the food to back it up. Shrimp, native blue crab, scallops, you name it, they have it, not to mention a heck of a great Happy Hour to go with it – including a doozy called Chatham Artillery Punch! They bake breads and desserts right there, and you can even purchase some to take to your room. Friends and family back home will be grateful if you take advantage of River House Seafood's dessert mail-order service.

For a more casual atmosphere you'll want to kick up your heels at **Spanky's Pizza Galley and Saloon**. Dubbed as the *"home of the original chicken finger"* and voted Savannah's best bar food, Spanky's has a loyal following of visitors and locals who can't get enough of their famous chicken fingers and spuds. Other items like nachos, pizza and burgers round out this feel-good menu where strangers quickly become friends in the midst of Spanky's laid-back atmosphere.

Everyone talks about Southern hospitality, and that sweetness has got to come from somewhere. Chances are, it is from the Savannah Candy Kitchen or River Street Sweets. Our best advice is to throw any ideas of a diet into the river and just indulge! From world-famous pralines to decadent fudge and so much more this is where candy land is redefined. One step into these shops of confectionary delights and even your sense of smell will develop a sweet tooth - yes, it's that good!

When the sun goes down, River Street calls to tourists and locals who want a good time and a good drink. Wet Willie's, at 101 East River Street, caters to the whole family during the day, with frozen, non-alcoholic beverages in a rainbow of colors and flavors. At night, however, it is adult swim. Savannah differs from its sister city, Charleston, in one way that visitors to our bars and pubs appreciate: you can take a plastic to-go cup outside and catch the sights while they're still in focus. So, if a local sees you on the street with a drink in hand and says, "I see a traveler" they aren't calling you out for your tourist status. That is simply the slang for the popular mobile cocktail you're carrying.

Savannah is a city influenced by the waters that surround it, and River Street is an eclectic product of the national and international guests who remain intrigued by it year after year. For more information, please visit the River Street Visitor Center, open from 10 a.m. to 10 p.m., seven days a week. ❋

# Georgia's Authentic Beach Town...
# Tybee Island

by Heather Grant

**Charming yet quirky**, Tybee may not fit the typical high-rise beach mold but that suits residents and visitors just fine.

Seeing the beautiful sites in Savannah may require a good pair of walking shoes, but just 20 minutes east of the city, you'll discover another great escape that is best experienced with no shoes at all – Tybee Island, Georgia. Unlike many coastal beaches you may have visited before, dotted with high-rise condominiums and theme parks, the people of Tybee Island have made it their mission to retain the nostalgia of days gone by for a truly laid back retreat. "Even today, many of the restaurants and hotels on Tybee are what we refer to as locally owned and grown," said Lindsay Fruchtl, marketing director for the **Tybee Island Tourism Council**. "You won't see many chains on the island and our visitors continue to be drawn to the uniqueness we offer," she added. Perhaps that's why Tybee Island was recently named one of *Travel + Leisure Magazine's* "Best Beach Towns," just one of many accolades the island receives year after year.

With a history that dates back to the 18th century, complete with lore of pirates and buried treasure, Tybee's five miles of uninterrupted beach didn't become a resort destination until 1887. At that time, Savannah's wealthy would visit the island, known as the community of "Ocean City," choosing to arrive either via a three-hour steamship voyage or two hours by train. Fast forward nearly 40 years and Tybee's palm-lined highway, which remains to this day as the island's sole access route, made it easy for beach-goers to bask in the warmth of the Southern sun. "It's difficult to come here and be stuffy and regimented," says George Spriggs Jr. of Tybee's North Beach Bar and Grill. "This place lends itself to shorts, flip flops, shirts - sometimes not [shirts] - and we don't move at a real quick pace," he adds with a knowing laugh.

Though the intentional absence of high-rise buildings on the island is a welcome sight, it may make you wonder where visitors actually stay. Even without multi-level structures, Tybee still offers more than 500 hotel rooms, all within one block of the beach, in addition to quaint ocean-side cottages, inns and bed and breakfast's, RV and camping grounds and rental properties for every price range. Without a doubt, there is no shortage of rooms to rest your head and fall asleep to the sound of crashing waves on Tybee. "Once [visitors] come they're coming back every year then before long

*Above:* The Tybee Island Pier and Pavilion may be a hot spot for activity, but just beneath this impressive structure you'll discover peace and quite like no other.

they're looking for a little place and then they become one of us," commented Ralph Douglas Jones of Fish Art on Tybee Island.

As you arrive on the island, if your idea of the perfect beach day includes planting a chair and yourself in the sand for hours on end, Tybee offers ample opportunity to do just that. Depending on where you are on the island, you can opt for a quiet secluded stretch of beach, or the daily attractions near the expansive Tybee Island Pier and Pavilion. For those who prefer a more active experience, Tybee also offers dolphin boat tours, deep-sea fishing excursions, kiteboarding lessons, kayaking, paddle boarding and more. Of course there are also those who are somewhere in between a beach bum and a go-getter and for you, there's souvenir shopping on Tybrisa Street at the north end of the island, and one-of-a-kind art galleries, like Tybee Oaks, which is full of work by local artisans, on the southern tip. "Tybee has its own identity, which is not branded by major corporations, it's a lot of really creative, small businesses," remarked Kurtis Schumm of the Tybee Island Social Club restaurant.

The Tybee Island Marine Science Center also offers visitors a unique glimpse at the aquatic life that calls this little island home. You'll discover what lies within Tybee's beaches, marshes and rivers through gallery and classroom experiences designed to enhance conservation and stewardship of coastal Georgia's natural resources.

Young and old, history buff or not, another must-see while visiting Tybee is the Tybee Island Light Station. Built in 1773, the Tybee lighthouse is the oldest and tallest in Georgia. Surrounded by the relatively flat expanse of land common to the area, you will experience the very best of breathtaking bird's eye views from atop the lighthouse – that is if 178 steps don't sound too imposing. After your inspiring climb, you can also enjoy the Tybee Museum and gift shop, which are both located on the premises and safely back on the ground.

© Bryan Stovall

*Above:* The Tybee Island Pier and Pavilion provides visitors with stunning views over the Atlantic Ocean and year-round activities.

**Without a doubt, as you feel the sand between your toes and hear the crash of the waves, looking out over a horizon that stretches as far as the eye can see, you, too, will be swept up in the authentic beach town of Tybee.**

Now that your exercise is done, it's time to eat! In keeping with its nostalgic feel, many of the restaurants on Tybee are also long-time establishments whose owners know how to cater to Tybee locals and visitors alike. Fresh seafood abounds at Tybee eateries, which include the Crab Shack, known by locals as the place where *"the elite eat in their bare feet"* complete with an outdoor alligator pond – kept at a safe distance of course. There's also A-J's Dockside, which offers stunning sunset views and a laid-back atmosphere, Macelwee's, the oldest continually operating restaurant on Tybee and North Beach Grill, where you can easily get swept away by the fun atmosphere and ocean breezes. You can also branch out and enjoy some emerging restaurants on the island such as the Tybee Island Social Club, which offers a new spin on old seafood favorites.

Another relative newcomer to the island is the Tybee Island Wedding Chapel. Originally built in 2009 by Disney Studios for use in the Miley Cyrus movie, *The Last Song,* this stunning chapel is now available for weddings and offers an unforgettable experience.

You may think that a major motion picture would draw quite a crowd to the island – and it did – but not as big as the annual parades for which Tybee is famous. Pull out your water guns at the Beach Bum festivities, which usher in summer over Memorial Day Weekend; flaunt your green best at the Irish Heritage Parade in celebration of St. Patrick; practice bead catching during the Mardi Gras celebration; and bring the whole family out for the Pirate Festival Parade in the fall where there's no shortage of fun for all. Christmas and New Year's celebrations (brace for the polar bear plunge!) are also island favorites along with a magical fireworks display that reflects in the waves of the Atlantic for Independence Day in July.

Though nostalgia runs deep on Tybee Island, progress has certainly continued over the years, but it is the kind of progress you don't notice, which is just the way Tybee likes to keep it. From restoring historic cottages to an entire movement in support of Tybee's historic Post Theater, the island continues to be the perfect compliment to Savannah. "We believe the less people notice our progress, the better we are doing," added Lindsay with the Tybee Tourism Council.

When it comes down to it, what you really want to know is, "Why Tybee?" Just ask Maria T. Procopio of the Tybee Island Marine Science Center who summed it up best when she said, "Because it's accessible, affordable and authentic." Without a doubt, as you feel the sand between your toes and hear the crash of the waves, looking out over a horizon that stretches as far as the eye can see, you, too, will be swept up in the authentic beach town of Tybee – all we can say is, join the club. ✤

# Sweet Savannah Movie Making

*by Heather Grant*

When he's not scooping ice cream, Savannah native Stratton Leopold is producing multi-million dollar Hollywood movies. Wait, did you get that? Let's try it one more time just in case – *Take two -- And action!* The same man who jubilantly scoops ice cream for patrons young and old also regularly hobnobs with the likes of Tom Cruise, Jennifer Anniston, Ben Affleck and dozens of other A-listers as a major motion picture producer – *And cut -- That's a wrap!* Actually, that's just the beginning…

If you have been to Leopold's Ice Cream on Broughton Street in Savannah (and if you haven't yet, you should) you may notice a certain movie theme that fills the establishment. There, in the midst of a dozen or more decadent ice cream varieties and full menu of items, you will see movie posters and memorabilia all of which hold a special place in Stratton's heart, much like his hometown.

"People really like Savannah – movie crews, actors, directors – they come here and they fall in love," said Stratton, former Vice President of Production for Paramount Pictures. Case in point, Academy Award® Winning Actor, Ben Affleck, still owns a home in the Savannah area years after discovering the city while filming *Forces of Nature* with Sandra Bulloch in 1999. Not only do movie crews have an eye for Savannah, but major retailors such as *Pottery Barn* have also used Savannah when photographing their product catalogs. Even the ABC series, *Extreme Makeover: Home Edition* selected a Savannah family to receive a brand new home in 2010 and spent weeks preplanning and filming in the city.

With movies like *The General's Daughter* starring John Travolta, *Forrest Gump* with Tom Hanks, *Something to Talk About* with Julia Roberts and most recently, *The Conspirator* directed by Robert Redford, and dozens more, all using Savannah as their backdrop, Stratton believes the city is certainly coming into its own as a premier movie location destination.

"In the late 80s early 90s, period movies where the big thing," commented Stratton, "and it made sense because of Savannah's history. But I think Savannah is poised to do well in modern-day films, too thanks to the resurgence of tourism and the revitalization of the city." Though Savannah may lack a major soundstage, Stratton says even if there were one here, the big movie companies would still use their own stages in Hollywood. According to Stratton, it is Savannah's organic, natural appeal that has kept actors, producers, directors and film crews coming back for more than 60 films and counting.

Today, Stratton is a freelance producer who still works on box office hits (and was recently on location in New Orleans with Jennifer Anniston and Jason Statham) but whose newfound passion is smaller, independent films. "Savannah is perfect for independent productions and that is my dream for this city."

The question remains, however, can you really mix ice cream and movie making? "I'm working on a new flavor with an Academy Award® Winning Actress right now," Stratton quips, "making movies and scooping ice cream – now that's my dream day!" ❁

---

## Savannah's Filmography

**Cape Fear**: Gregory Peck, Robert Mitchum and Polly Bergen *(1962)*

**The Longest Yard**: Burt Reynolds *(1974)*

**Gator**: Burt Reynolds *(1976)*

**Glory**: Denzel Washington *(1989)*

**Camilla**: Jessica Tandy, Bridget Fonda *(1993)*

**Forrest Gump**: Tom Hanks, Sally Field *(1994)*

**Now and Then**: Demi Moore, Rosie O'Donnell, Melanie Griffith, Rita Wilson, and Christina Ricci *(1995)*

**Something to Talk About**: Julia Roberts, Dennis Quaid *(1995)*

**Midnight in the Garden of Good and Evil**: Clint Eastwood, director *(1997)*

**The Gingerbread Man**: Kenneth Branagh, Embeth Davidtz, Robert Downey, Jr. *(1997)*

**The General's Daughter**: John Travolta *(1998)*

**Forces of Nature**: Sandra Bullock, Ben Affleck *(1999)*

**The Legend of Bagger Vance**: Matt Damon, Will Smith, Charlize Theron *(2000)*

**The Gift**: Cate Blanchett, Keanu Reeves, Katie Holmes *(2000)*

**The Haunted Mansion**: Eddie Murphy *(2003)*

**The Last Song**: Miley Cyrus, Greg Kinnear *(2010)*

**The Conspirator**: Robert Redford, director with Justin Long, Evan Rachel Wood and Robin Wright Penn *(2010)*

*For more information on Stratton's body of work, please visit imdb.com keyword: Stratton Leopold.*

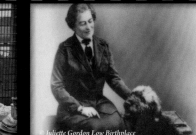
© Juliette Gordon Low Birthplace

© Bryan Stovall

# Savannah's Famous Folks

## From Notable Figures to Pop Icons, Savannah Natives are Still Making History

**Billy Currington.** *(1973 -)* Country music fans will quickly recognize the name of this Savannah native who was born in the city and raised a mere 30 minutes away in Rincon, Georgia. With song lyrics like, "God is great, beer is good and people are crazy," Billy has quickly made a name for himself on the worldwide country music scene earning him ten Top 10 hits with six of those hitting No. 1. Since his debut in 2003, Billy has toured with such well -known artists as Kenny Chesney, Brad Paisley, Sugarland and Carrie Underwood.

**Charles Coburn.** *(1877-1961)* With an Academy Award®, over 40 movie roles and a star on the Hollywood Walk of Fame to his name, Coburn was an actor much beloved for his comedic roles and smooth, low voice.

**Clarence Thomas.** *(1948-)* Born just outside of Savannah in the small settlement of Pinpoint, Georgia, Justice Thomas was appointed a U.S. Supreme Court Judge in 1991—becoming the second African-American to take a seat on the country's highest court.

**Conrad Aiken.** *(1889-1973)* Born in a house near Savannah's Colonial Park Cemetery, the poet spent much of his childhood in Massachusetts after the murder-suicide of his father and mother. Following a successful writing career that had him named Poetry Consultant to the Library of Congress, Aiken returned to his beloved Hostess City. He is buried at Bonaventure Cemetery under a bench engraved with the intriguingly poetic epilogue "Cosmos Mariner, Destination Unknown."

**Flannery O'Connor.** *(1925-1964)* A writer of the dark but humorous Southern Gothic genre, O'Connor spent the first formative years of her life at 207 East Charlton Street. Today, the modest home in the shadow of the Cathedral of St. John the Baptist is open to the public as a museum dedicated to the author's early life. Visitors can even enjoy a bit of shade in the very backyard where O'Connor is known to have trained a chicken to walk backwards.

**Johnny Mercer.** *(1909-1976)* Arguably the most famous and beloved of all Savannahians, the prolific singer/songwriter and co-founder of Capitol Records penned some of America's favorite songs, including "Come Rain or Come Shine," "Skylark," "Jeepers Creepers," "You Must Have Been a Beautiful Baby," and "Moon River." Mercer's talent earned him four Academy Awards® and a bronze statue in Ellis Square. *(above right)*

**Juliette Gordon Low.** *(1860-1927)* The founder of the Girl Scouts of the U.S.A., "Daisy," as she was known to family and friends, spent most of her life in Savannah and used the city as a home base for her burgeoning organization. Today, there are two historic sites in the city involving the philanthropist and female empowerment activist: The Juliette Gordon Low Birthplace at 10 East Oglethorpe and the Girl Scout's First Headquarters at 330 Drayton Street. *(above middle)*

**Mitchell Hall and April Johnston.** On *Bravo Channel's* hit series *Project Runway*, up-and-coming fashion designers compete each week for the chance to become the new "it" designer. In recent seasons, two Savannah natives, Mitchell Hall (season 6) and April Johnston (season 8) have both starred on the reality show with April being the youngest designer to compete in the show's history.

**Paula Deen.** *(1947-)* Iconic restaurateur, cookbook author and *Food Network* star got her start on the southside of Savannah making box lunches for office folks. Famous for her love of real Southern cooking and unapologetic use of butter, Paula films many of her shows at her residence on Wilmington Island, where she lives with her boat captain husband, Michael Groover. *(above left)*

**Ruby Gettinger.** *(1975-)* Charming and compassionate, Ruby's self-titled *Style Network* reality show has become a runaway hit its past two seasons. Folks from all over the world have fallen in love with this redhead working to reach a healthy weight with humor and honesty while providing indefatigable inspiration to all.

**Uga.** *(mascot for the University of Georgia)* Since 1956, the lineage of English Bulldog mascots for the University of Georgia have all been descendants of a local Savannah family. Frank W. "Sonny" Seiler, local celebrity and lawyer, and his family are the caretakers of this popular "dawg" and are present with the reigning Uga at Georgia Bulldogs' home football games, away games and special University-related events. With his air-conditioned doghouse and bed made of ice, Uga is one hot mascot who knows how to keep his cool. ❀

# That's Entertainment

## HOME TO THE OLDEST CONTINUALLY OPERATING THEATRE IN THE NATION, SAVANNAH DEFINITELY KNOWS HOW TO PUT ON A SHOW

*by Heather Grant*

Though the seats are likely filled with a diverse crowd, as the lights dim and the performance begins, everyone is united in a collective sense of anticipation. Soon, swept up in the talents on display, you unknowingly escape the real world and find yourself completely enthralled and joyfully exhilarated. From musical theater to pop-music concerts, variety acts to dramatic plays, **Savannah's theatres and performing art centers offer a range of entertaining options designed for your ultimate delight.**

### Savannah Theatre

On December 4, 1818, the **Savannah Theatre** opened its doors for the very first time at the corner of Bull and West McDonough Streets, offering audience members the chance to see live performances that were both comedic and dramatic. In the mid-20th century, this illustrious theatre, originally designed by William Jay, the same architect responsible for the Telfair Mansion, was converted into a motion picture house. During this time, in 1948, a devastating fire ravaged the theatre but it was eventually brought back to life reflective of the 1940s Art-Deco style that remains the theatre's signature look to this very day. In 2002, a massive restoration project was completed including state-of-the-art lighting and sound, while still keeping the building's historic ambiance in tact. Among those who have performed at the historic theatre throughout its nearly 200-year history are W.C. Fields and Edwin Booth, brother of John Wilkes Booth. Audiences at the theatre can now choose from an ongoing variety of live musical performances with actors who dance and sing their way into your heart through Southern favorites, hits of the 50s, 60s, 70s and 80s and even a seasonal Christmas show. "The Savannah Theatre offers superior entertainment for visitors of all ages," said Linda Harris, director of sales and marketing for the theatre. "Our two-hour musicals are based on different genres of music from past and present decades offering year-round performances." If you're near Chippewa Square, stop by the box office to find out more about the theatre's performance schedule or simply go online. (*savannahtheatre.com*)

### Lucas Theatre

Even though co-designer, Arthur Lucas, owned more than 20 theatres throughout the south at the time, the Lucas Theatre in Savannah is the only one that reflects his name. Built in 1921 by Lucas and architect C.K. Howell, in its heyday, the theatre was the epicenter of entertainment for Savannah and a hot spot for traveling road shows. After losing its audience to the popularity of TV, the theatre closed in 1976 and over the next 10 years was threatened with demolition multiple times. Thankfully, in 1986, a group of citizens banned together and bought the building. By 2002, and $14 million later, the Lucas reopened and today is under the care and operation of the Savannah College of Art and Design. Operas, orchestras, music stars and more now regularly perform at the Lucas throughout the year breathing new life into the historic building and all who enter it. *(lucastheatre.com)*

### Trustees Theater

Originally constructed as a "completely new and modern motion picture theater," The Trustees Theater was the first in the southeast to be built with air conditioning that was adjustable to audiences' needs. The theater doors officially opened for the first time on February 14, 1946 and seated 1,200 audience members for both motion picture and theatrical performances. After a hugely successful run, the theater closed due to lack of patrons in 1980 but was acquired by the Savannah College of Art and Design in 1989 for use by its various student shows and needs. It wasn't until 1998, with an opening performance by singer Tony Bennett, that the establishment reopened as

the Trustees Theater, which today hosts performances, concerts and lectures throughout the year and has contributed greatly to the resurgence of live theater in downtown Savannah. *(trusteestheater.com)*

### The Savannah Civic Center

With its modern edge and historic location, the Savannah Civic Center offers something for everyone in search of live entertainment. Built in 1974, the Civic Center is a multi-purpose arena located on Montgomery Street in historic downtown. From circus acts and rousing concerts held in the 9,600-seat Martin Luther King, Jr. Arena to the more intimate performances of the 2,524-seat Johnny Mercer Theater, the Civic Center maintains a full roster of performances throughout the year. Annual events such as the Savannah Tire Hockey Classic, the Junior League Thrift Sale, and various other trade shows and public events are also held at the center attracting huge crowds. *(savannahcivic.com)* ❈

© Bryan Stovall

*Opposite:* The **Savannah Theatre** may be the oldest continually operating of its kind, but its energetic performances are appealing to audiences with newfound excitement. *(see ad page 51)*

*Above:* The Lucas Theatre, now owned and operated by SCAD, reopened in 2002 after a $14 million renovation.

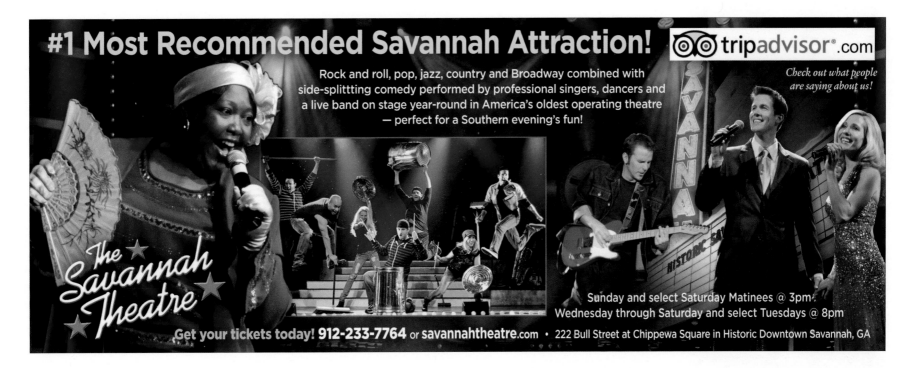

# Celebrations for All Seasons

© Savannah Riverfront, The "Peacemaker" Tall Ship

© Frank Stewart, John Pizzarelli

© Visit Savannah, St. Patrick's Day Parade

## ❋ YEAR 'ROUND

### River Street Festivals
*Throughout 2012*
*912.234.0295 | riverstreetsavannah.com*
No matter what time of year, River Street has a festival to celebrate: Each month, First Friday fireworks bring new meaning to TGIF, followed by the family fun and bustling art scene of First Saturdays. Practically every culture gets its due on the Riverfront's historic cobblestoned streets through the seasons, from the German food and songs of Oktoberfest to June's spicy Fiesta Latina to one of the biggest, greenest St. Patrick's Day celebrations in the nation. Fine Arts on the River showcases visual and performing arts and Christmas on the River is as fine a Savannah tradition as they come. Events are always family friendly!

## ❋ JANUARY

### Annual MLK Jr. Observance Day Celebration
*912.234.5502 | savannahga.gov*

### Savannah Tire Hockey Classic
*912.644.6414 | savannahhockeyclassic.com*

## ❋ FEBRUARY

### Savannah Black Heritage Festival
*February 1-16, 2012*
*912.358.4309 | savannahblackheritagefestival.com*
African-American art, gospel music and Gullah-Geechee storytelling entertain while health-related and economic programming inform. Events take place all over the city. This year's theme is *Journeys, Passages and Transitions* and is certain to be another exceptional festival.

### Savannah Book Festival
*February 15-19, 2012*
*912.358.0575 | savannahbookfestival.org*
Literati from near and far convene in Savannah each year for lectures, books signings and workshops led by experts and authors in all of the top genres including fiction, history, biography, poetry and beyond. The 2012 Fest features a keynote address by noted author, Mr. Pat Conroy. Visit the website to see if your favorite author is making an appearance and while there make a note of events that SBF organizers host throughout the year.

### Georgia History Festival
*912.651.2125 | georgiahistory.com*

### Savannah Irish Festival
*912.232.3448 | savannahirish.org*

### Super Museum Sunday
*912.651.2125 | georgiahistory.com*

## ❋ MARCH

### St. Patrick's Day
*March 17, 2012*
*912.233.4804 | savannahsaintpatricksday.com*
More than just a day, St. Patrick's Day in Savannah is a citywide event where the population nearly doubles in size as honorary Irish descend on the city. The festivities begin days before the actual holiday arrives but on the 17th, the fun kicks off with the largest parade in the southeast. Even after the last float glides by the celebration continues on River Street, in City Market and on the beaches of Tybee Island.

### Savannah Music Festival
*March 22-April 7, 2012*
*912.525.5050 | savannahmusicfestival.org*
From avant garde jazz and bluegrass to symphonic classics to rock n' roll, the Savannah Music Festival (SMF) leaves no aural stone unturned. Renowned internationally for its breadth of scope and quality of artists, the multiple stages of this event have featured the likes of Stuart Copeland, Bela Fleck, Wilco, Angelique Kidjo and Savannah's own Ben Tucker. SMF commissions original work each year, premiering pieces by global artists heard publically for the first time in Savannah.

### Savannah Tour of Homes and Gardens
*912.234.8054 | savannahtourofhomes.org*

### Tara Feis Festival
*912.651.6417 | savannahga.gov*

### Tybee Island's St. Patrick's Heritage Celebration Parade
*912.786.5444 | tybeevisit.com*

## ❋ APRIL

### Liberty Mutual Legends of Golf, PGA Champions Tour
*April 16-22, 2012*
*912.236.1333 | lmlog.com*
See the greatest legends of the game up close and in person at what has fast become Savannah's favorite new tradition. Held at The Club at Savannah Harbor, you'll enjoy the beauty of this immaculate course and the expertise that has made these players true legends of the game.

### North of Gwinnett Street (NOGS) Tour of Hidden Gardens
*912.961.4805 | gcofsavnogstour.org*

### Savannah Garden Exposition
*912.236.4795 | savannahgardenexpo.com*

### SCAD International Festival
*912.525.5231 | scad.edu*

### SCAD Sidewalk Arts Festival
*912.525.5231 | scad.edu*

### Spring Fling Art and Music Festival
*912.786.5444 | tybeevisit.com*

## ❋ MAY

### Tall Ships Challenge
*May 3-7, 2012*
*912.234.0295 | savannahtallshipschallenge.com*
Up to 15 tall ships will dock in Savannah as part of the "Tall Ships Challenge 2012, Atlantic Coast" race, which starts in Jacksonville, Florida in late April, before arriving in Savannah. The ships race to a buoy in the ocean on May 3 and then gather as they enter the port under full sail in what can only be described as an impressive parade like no other.

### Fine Arts on the River Festival
*912.234.0295 | riverstreetsavannah.com*

### SCAD Sand Arts Festival
*912.525.5231 | scad.edu*

### Savannah Scottish Games
*912.233.6017 | savannahscottishgames.com*

### Savannah Shakespeare Festival
*912.651.6417 | savannahga.gov*

### Tybee Island Beach Bum Parade
*912.786.5444 | tybeevisit.com*

## JUNE

### Armed Forces Festival on River Street
*912.234.0295 | riverstreetsavannah.com*

### Fiesta Latina
*912.651.6417 | savannahga.gov*

### Savannah Asian Festival
*912.651.6417 | savannahga.gov*

## ❋ JULY

### Fourth of July
*July 4, 2012*
*912.234.0295 | riverstreetsavannah.com*
*877.339.9330 | tybeevisit.com*
Whether you prefer your fireworks over the river or reflecting in the Atlantic Ocean (or both!) Savannah puts on quite an Independence Day Celebration each year. The festivities begin on Tybee Island with a breathtaking fireworks display over the Atlantic Ocean. Patriotism then flows over to River Street where an equally impressive show of pyrotechnics can be seen from both River Street and Hutchinson Island.

## ❋ AUGUST

### Savannah Craft Brew Fest
*August 31-September 2, 2012*
*877.SAVANNAH | savannahcraftbrewfest.com*
These folks elevate beer drinking to an art form when more than 120 microbrew companies bring their wares to the Savannah International Trade &Convention Center for Labor Day Weekend. Brews are matched with the finest Lowcountry cuisine to bring out their best flavors at the Craft Brew Pairings dinner on Friday night, followed by an all-day bonanza Saturday with entertainment, excellent eats and of course, plenty of taxis so no one needs to drive home.

Throughout the year Savannah is host to dozens of festivals that celebrate culture, art, music and always fun. Below is a listing of events planned for 2012. We encourage you to refer to *VisitSavannah.com* for a comprehensive listing of events and more detailed information.

### ❈ September

**Taste of Savannah**
*September 14, 2012*
912.232.1223 | *tasteofsavannah.org*
Each year the Savannah Area Tourism Leadership Council hosts what has quickly become a must-experience event to sample the best of Savannah cuisine. The annual Taste of Savannah is held each year at the Savannah International Trade and Convention Center where more than 25 restaurants assemble in one place to give attendees the chance to taste their way through the city's finest eateries. From savory entrees to decadent desserts, all accompanied by live musical entertainment, guests are always sure to satisfy their appetite for good food and an even better time.

**Savannah Jazz Festival**
912.651.6783 | *savannahjazzfestival.org*
Savannah always cools off for fall with a week of free music events sponsored by the city, most taking place on the amphitheater stage in Forsyth Park. From Dixieland and swing to downhome "gutbucket" blues and the swirly stylings of modern contemporary masters, Jazz Fest brings together every genre to appeal to all ages and tastes. No need for tickets – just grab a cooler and a folding chair and you're good to go! *(check website for exact dates)*

**Labor Day Beach Bash**
912.786.5393 | *tybeefest.com*

**Savannah Ocean Exchange**
*savannahoceanexchange.org*

### ❈ October

**Savannah Film Festival**
912.525.5231 | *filmfest.scad.edu*
The Savannah College of Art and Design brings Hollywood to Savannah with screenings of the best independent films from around the world. Big-time directors share screen time with student filmmakers to showcase shorts, features and documentaries, many of which go on to become box-office smashes. Celebrities tend to find their way to town during this time, transforming Savannah into Los Angeles for a short while, paparazzi and all. *(check website for exact dates)*

**Tybee Island Pirate Festival**
*877.339.9330* | *tybeeisland.com/piratefest*
Arrrgh ya' ready for some marauding and mischief?! Tybee Island celebrates the high-flying antics of history's friendly buccaneers with a weekend of treasure hunting at the Thieves' Market, a costumed gala, activities for the little mates, a parade where pirates share their booty with the crowd and a music festival that ye landlubbers have ne'er experienced. *(check website for exact dates)*

**Oktoberfest on the River**
912.234.0295 | *riverstreetsavannah.com*

**Picnic in the Park**
912.651.6417 | *savannahga.gov/arts*

**St. Vincent's Academy Tour of Homes and Tea**
912.819.7780 | *svatourofhomes.com*

**Savannah Folk Music Festival**
912.786.6953 | *savannahfolk.org*

**Savannah Greek Festival**
912.236.8256 | *stpaulsgreekorthodox.org*

**Shalom Y'all Jewish Food Festival**
912.233.1547 | *mickveisrael.org*

**Tybee Festival of the Arts**
912.786.5920 | *tybeearts.org/festival*

### ❈ November

**Rock n' Roll Marathon**
*877.SAVANNAH* | *runrocknroll.competitor.com/savannah*
2011 marked the first year for this national and international marathon sensation to hit Savannah and it sold out! With its scenic route through Savannah dotted with the heart-pumping live music from today's hottest musical bands, the Rock n' Roll Marathon is destined to become a long-lasting Savannah event.

**Savannah Harbor Boat Parade of Lights**
912.201.2000 | *westinsavannah.com*

**Savannah Holly Days**
912.644.6452 | *savannahhollydays.com*

**Savannah Seafood Festival**
912.234.0295 | *riverstreetsavannah.com*

**Telfair Art Fair**
912.790.8800 | *telfair.org*

### ❈ December

**City Market Christmas and New Year's Eve Celebrations**
912.232.4903 | *savannahcitymarket.com*
The holidays are a very special time of year for the merchants and visitors of city market. Trees are illuminated with white lights, crisp evergreen and bright red bows adorn every shop and even Father Christmas comes for a visit. Specific events include a Holiday Open House and Christmas for Kids Celebration. As New Year's Eve approaches, City Market plays host to an outdoor street party that keeps visitors dancing to live musical entertainment.

**Christmas on the River and Lighted Holiday Parade**
912.234.0295 | *riverstreetsavannah.com*

**ENMARK Savannah River Bridge Run**
912.355.3527 | *savannahriverbridgerun.com*

**Holiday Tour of Homes**
912.236.8362 | *dnaholidaytour.com*

**Tybee New Year's Eve Fireworks**
912.786.5444 | *tybeevisit.com* ❈

"SMF is one of the best music festivals in the country... keeping the world safe for good, live music."
*—Charleston Post & Courier*

**SAVANNAH MUSIC FESTIVAL**
MARCH 22–APRIL 7, 2012 | MARCH 21–APRIL 6, 2013

JAZZ CLASSICAL AMERICANA WORLD MUSIC
For Tickets: www.savannahmusicfestival.org or (912) 525-5050

SPONSORED BY: The City of Savannah Dept. of Cultural Affairs • Gulfstream Aerospace Corp. • Visit Savannah
Memorial Health University Medical Center/Mercer University School of Medicine • Savannah College of Art & Design • Telfair Museums
Connect Savannah • Critz Inc. • Wet Willie's Management Corp. • Audi Hilton Head • The Kennickell Group • Savannah Morning News
AT&T Advertising Solutions • Comcast • Hunter Maclean • GPB Media • WTOC • Adventure Radio

© Mighty Eighth Air Force Museum

## Prepare for Take Off!

# Fun for the Whole Family

WHETHER YOU'RE YOUNG OR JUST YOUNG AT HEART,
SAVANNAH IS FULL OF ACTIVITIES THAT WILL MAKE TRAVELERS OF ALL AGES HAPPY CAMPERS (*NO REAL CAMPING REQUIRED*).

*by Heather Grant*

## Fly a B-17 Bomber

*175 Bourne Avenue in Pooler | 912.748.8888 | mightyeighth.org*

The interactive flight simulator at the Mighty Eighth Air Force Museum will take you on a journey through time with its engine roar and flashing cockpit. The simulator, which is part of a dramatic 90,000 square-foot installation, was built to honor Air Force veterans of WWII and "edutain" (that's educate and entertain) generations about the heroics of these valiant men and women. The second floor of the museum displays authentic war regalia, including a dog-tag machine, while the Combat Gallery boasts a fleet of restored aircraft that were used in battle giving visitors the rare opportunity to stand next to an authentic B-17 Bomber.

## Commune with Nature

*52 Diamond Causeway | 800.864.7275 | gastateparks.org/SkidawayIsland*

Miles of hiking and biking trails wind through salt marshes and maritime forests within the 588 acres of Skidaway Island State Park. Whether you're making it a day trip or packing a tent for bona fide camping, be on the lookout for the park's many animal residents including deer, fiddler crabs, egrets and flocks of migrating birds. The interpretive center at the ranger's station has a birding station, a reptile room and other natural and cultural exhibits.

## Dine with Pirates

*20 East Broad Street | 912.233.5757 | thepirateshouse.com*

Legend has it that Captain Flint from the Robert Louis Stevenson classic *Treasure Island* died in an upstairs room at what is now **The Pirates' House Restaurant** with first mate, Billy Bones, at his side. This landmark eatery opened in 1753 as an inn for seafarers—you can still explore the tunnel where unsuspecting sailors were shanghaied onto pirate ships. Keep your eyes open for pirates in the dining room ready to pose for photos between courses!

*Aaargh mateys!*

## Cozy Up with a Wolf

*711 Sandtown Road | 912.395.1212 | oatlandisland.org*

Just minutes from downtown, the Wolf Wilderness habitat at Oatland Island Wildlife Center gives folks nose-to-nose access with a pack of gray wolves (with a thick Plexiglass window in between, of course). The air-conditioned wolf observation cabin is part of an easy two-mile nature trail that winds through lush Lowcountry forest and serene marsh past bison, panthers, owls, eagles, farm animals and other local flora and fauna. In fall 2011, the Center added Southern Flying Squirrels to the Wolf Exhibit (albeit with separate living quarters) giving visitors a fun view of these fascinating nocturnal gliders.

*Hoooowll!*

## Touch a Sand Dollar

*1510 Strand Avenue, Tybee Island | 912.786.5917 | tybeemarinescience.org*

Depending on the day, the touch tank at the Tybee Island Marine Science Center is swimming with creatures native to the Georgia Coast, including whelk, hermit crabs, starfish and more. Learn about the tides, reefs, dolphins and life cycles of sea turtles that nest on our local beaches. The center also offers guided beach walks, marsh treks and a gift shop full of fluffy critters to take home!

*Hands-on Learning!*

## Be an Architect

*207 W. York Street Savannah | 912.790.8800 | telfair.org*

You can build a likeness of one of Savannah's historic homes or create something no one's ever seen before with the blocks at **ArtZeum at Telfair Museum's Jepson Center for the Arts**. The two-level, 3500 square-foot gallery has plenty more to keep those little hands busy, including a magnetic sculpture wall and other interactive exhibits using works from the Telfair collection.

*Discover Your True Colors!*

## Explore a Fort

*U.S. 80 East | 912.786.5787 | nps.gov/fopu*

As you walk through the cannonball-shattered walls of Fort Pulaski National Monument, it's a cinch to imagine what it was like to guard the Savannah River way back when. Built in 1847, the fort was used by the Confederacy and thought to be impenetrable until the Union Army tested its new rifled canon in 1862, rendering brick forts everywhere obsolete. After you've strolled through both levels, check out the visitors' center's films and live demonstrations as well as the moat, drawbridge and network of wooded trails. Keep your eyes peeled for a deer or a bald eagle—or, considering its haunted reputation, maybe even the ghost of a Confederate soldier.

© Bryan Stovall

Walk Through History!

© Savannah Sand Gnats

Gnate the Gnat!

## Catch a Fly Ball

*1401 Victory Road | 912.351.9150 | sandgnats.com*

Baseball legends Hank Aaron and Babe Ruth have scuffed their cleats at historic Grayson Stadium, home to the beloved **Savannah Sand Gnats**. A friendly crowd cheers for the home team while enjoying comfortable seating, gourmet treats and fireworks (the selection of micro-brews make this an excellent grown-up outing, too!) Don't forget to high-five the team mascot, Gnate the Gnat.

## Earn a Badge

*10 E. Oglethorpe Avenue | 912.233.4502 | girlscouts.org/birthplace*

Welcome to the **Juliette Gordon Low Birthplace**, otherwise known as "Girl Scouts Mecca." Thankfully you don't have to sport a sash to appreciate the legacy of a woman called "Daisy" who launched the organization to empower young girls and improve the world (the cookies came later). Enthusiastic guides know every nook and cranny of the elegant 1821 home, which is furnished with nineteenth-century pieces from the family's personal collection.

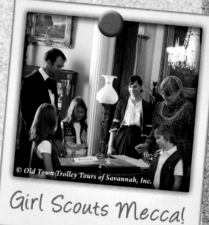

© Old Town Trolley Tours of Savannah, Inc.

Girl Scouts Mecca!

© UGA Marine Education Center and Aquarium

Look at the fish!

## See Science in Action

*30 Ocean Science Circle | 912.598.2496 | marex.uga.edu.*

The scientists at the UGA Marine Education Center and Aquarium on Skidaway Island are delighted to share their findings with visitors. A premier marine science research facility, the educational complex features 14 saltwater aquaria, interactive exhibits and a wheelchair accessible boardwalk around the marsh.

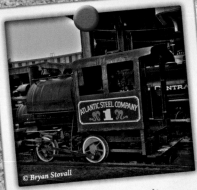

All Aboard!

© Bryan Stovall

## Ride a Locomotive

*601 W. Harris Street | 912.651.6823*

*chsgeorgia.org*

Going for a spin takes on a whole new meaning at **The Georgia State Railroad Museum**. Here, a giant turntable still shifts rail cars onto tracks just as it did years ago. Little engineers can learn about the history of steam engines and belt-driven machinery, and model train buffs will kick up their heels at the huge display of downtown Savannah! The museum is open daily, but train rides are seasonal—call ahead to check the schedule. Families will find even more to do at this historical complex run by the **Coastal Heritage Society**, including exploration of the **Savannah History Museum & Battlefield Memorial Park** and lunch at the **WhistleStop Café**. Phase one of two of the **Savannah Children's Museum** will also open in Spring 2012.

## Go Out with a Bang

*1 Fort Jackson Road | 912.232.3945*

*chsgeorgia.org*

Hear the awesome thunder of cannon fire at **Old Fort Jackson**, one of only eight "second system" fortifications built prior to the War of 1812 still standing in the U.S. The **Coastal Heritage Society** maintains the Visitor's Center featuring an exhibit of historical weapons and a host of highly entertaining guides dressed in period garb. ❊

Relive the Past!

© Bryan Stovall

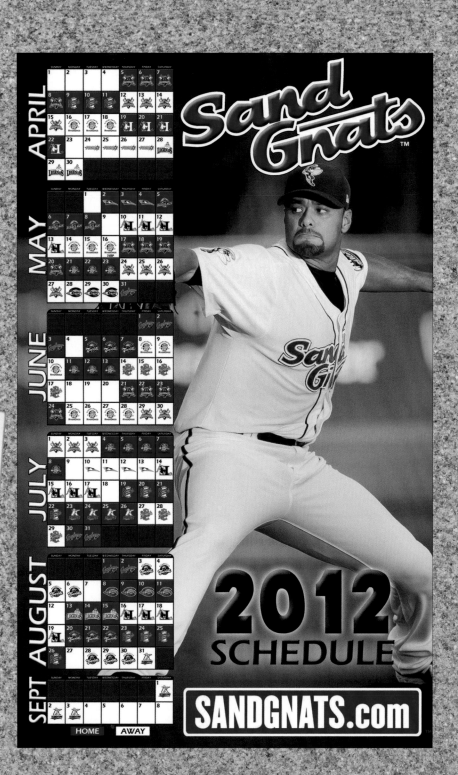

©Bryan Stovall

# HOSTESS CITY WELCOME

## DISCOVER SAVANNAH'S HOUSE MUSEUMS AND HISTORIC SITES. *by Allison Hersh*

One of Savannah's biggest attractions is its rich history, from the city's founding in 1733 through the Civil War and beyond. With three centuries of American history tucked beneath picturesque moss-draped squares and nestled along scenic local rivers, the area's house museums and historic sites attract visitors from near and far.

Savannah's National Landmark Historic District, which is one of the largest in the United States, offers 2.2 square miles filled with architectural gems. Visitors can discover Federal, Victorian, Gothic Revival and English Regency styles, with many homes open to the public year-round.

"The quality, integrity and diversity of Savannah's architecture is incredible," said Daniel Carey, president and CEO of **Historic Savannah Foundation**, a leading preservation organization

committed to preserving and protecting Savannah's heritage. "We have 18th, 19th and 20th century architecture that is well-cared for and illustrative of each of these periods."

The city features a wide range of house museums and historic sites open for daily tours. "We take our Hostess City label very seriously," said Carey. "There is a strong preservation ethos here that runs generations deep."

Here is a handy overview of some of Savannah's finest house museums and historic sites, organized by areas of interest. Don't miss the opportunity to explore the city's architectural and cultural treasures. There truly is something for everyone!

## For Literature Lovers

**Flannery O'Connor Home**

*207 E. Charlton Street | 912.233.6014 | flanneryoconnorhome.org*

The Flannery O'Connor Childhood Home is dedicated to preserving the legacy of one of the South's greatest writers. This 1856 home overlooking Lafayette Square has been meticulously restored to reflect the authentic period furnishings of a Depression-era rowhouse and to offer insight into the years that O'Connor lived in Savannah, from 1925 to 1938. This house museum displays many items from the writer's childhood, including her monogrammed baby carriage and an extensive library once owned by her family. The Flannery O'Connor Childhood Home also presents special events throughout the year, from free lectures to writing workshops.

## For Believers in the Supernatural

**Sorrel-Weed House**

*6 W. Harris Street | 912.236.8888 | sorrelweedhouse.com*

The Sorrel-Weed House, a stately 1840 antebellum mansion on Madison Square, is considered to be one of the region's finest examples of Greek Revival and Regency architecture. Featured on the *SyFy Channel's Ghost Hunters*, this mansion also enjoys a reputation as one of Savannah's most haunted houses. Francis Sorrel's wife committed suicide by jumping from the home's second floor porch in 1861. A slave also died a tragic death later that year, with both ghosts allegedly making periodic appearances at this historic home. History tours and paranormal tours are available daily. Also featured on *HGTV's If Walls Could Talk* and the *History Channel*, this structure is one of the first houses in Georgia to be named a state landmark and has hosted illustrious visitors like General William T. Sherman and General Robert E. Lee over the years.

© Bryan Stovall

## For Architecture Aficionados

**Harper Fowlkes House**

*230 Barnard Street | 912.234.2180 | harperfowlkeshouse.com*

The Harper Fowlkes House, located on Orleans Square, was originally built in 1842 and serves as a stately example of 19th century architecture. Topped with a distinctive mansard roof, the Harper Fowlkes House has served as the headquarters for the Society of the Cincinnati in the State of Georgia since local preservationist Alida Harper Fowlkes bequeathed the house to the organization in 1985. The house features a stunning assortment of original art and antiques offering insight into the life of Alida Harper, including her affinity for the arts. Landscape architect John McEllen designed the courtyard garden, which features a copper eagle sculpture as well as a red maple grown from a seed from George Washington's Virginia estate, Mount Vernon.

**Davenport House Museum**

*324 E. State Street | 912.236.8097 | davenporthousemuseum.org*

The **Davenport House Museum**, a property of **Historic Savannah Foundation**, on Columbia Square dates back to 1820 and has been meticulously restored to its original grandeur after being saved from demolition by a group of seven dedicated local women who formed the core of Historic Savannah Foundation in the 1950s. This once-neglected Federal-style brick structure, which officially launched the historic preservation movement in Savannah, is now a popular house museum where docents in period dress interpret the life of an early 19th century Savannah family.

**Owens-Thomas House**

*124 Abercorn Street | 912.233.9743 | telfair.org*

Elegance reigns supreme at the **Owens-Thomas House**, which is widely considered the finest example of English Regency architecture in America. Designed by acclaimed British architect William Jay, this National Historic Landmark overlooking Oglethorpe Square is one of three Telfair Museums' landmark buildings in Savannah. The home's collection of neoclassical furnishings, English-inspired parterre garden and original carriage house attract visitors from around the world. The carriage house contains one of the earliest intact urban slave quarters in the South, offering a fascinating glimpse into Savannah's past.

*Opposite:* The **Owens-Thomas House** is a fine example of English Regency architecture and a popular stop for visitors. *(see ad page 69)* **Left:** The **Davenport House Museum** officially launched the preservation movement in Savannah after it was saved from demolition. *(see ad page 24)*

© Bryan Stovall

© Historic Savannah Foundation

*Above:* The **Andrew Low House** was the adult home of Girl Scout's founder, Juliette Gordon Low and was also frequented by General Robert E. Lee. *(see ad page 24) Right:* The **Juliette Gordon Low Birthplace** hosts legions of Girl Scouts throughout the year. *(see ad page 24) Opposite:* Still standing since 1847, Fort Pulaski National Monument is a landmark brick fortress that played a key role during the Civil War.

## ▓ FOR GIRL SCOUTS FANS

### Juliette Gordon Low Birthplace

*10 E. Oglethorpe Avenue  |  912.233.4501  |  juliettegordonlowbirthplace.org*

Savannah's first designated National Historic Landmark site, the **Juliette Gordon Low Birthplace**, offers a lively tribute to Juliette Gordon Low, a.k.a. "Daisy," who founded the Girl Scouts of the USA on site in 1912. Originally built by Savannah mayor and U.S. Supreme Court Justice James Moore Wayne in 1818, this English Regency style mansion includes many historic artifacts from Daisy's life as well as spectacular period antiques. The home showcases a number of original paintings and sculpture by Juliette Gordon Low as well as a pair of iron gates she crafted by hand.

### Andrew Low House

*329 Abercorn Street  |  912.233.6854  |  andrewlowhouse.com*

Juliette's Gordon Low's home in adulthood, the **Andrew Low House** on Lafayette Square, is filled with antique furniture and other items belonging to this influential Savannah family. Visitors can follow in the footsteps of General Robert E. Lee, who was a frequent guest in the home. This signature structure overlooking Lafayette Square is a popular stop for Girl Scout troops visiting Savannah and is owned and operated by the National Society of The Colonial Dames of America in the State of Georgia.

## ▓ FOR "MIDNIGHT" FANS

### Mercer House

*429 Bull Street  |  912.238.0208  |  mercerhouse.com*

The Mercer House, the former home of local antiques dealer and preservationist Jim Williams, plays a central role in John Berendt's bestseller, *Midnight in the Garden of Good and Evil* and the movie of the same name, directed by Clint Eastwood. Originally designed in 1860 for Hugh W. Mercer, the great-grandfather of Academy Award® Winning songwriter Johnny Mercer, this brick mansion anchors Monterey Square and is open for daily tours. The home includes an extensive collection of antiques, while the carriage house fronting Whitaker Street houses a popular local gift shop.

## ▓ FOR TRAIN ENTHUSIASTS

### Georgia State Railroad Museum

*601 W. Harris Street  |  912.651.6823  |  chsgeorgia.org*

The **Georgia State Railroad Museum** stands apart as the largest and most complete antebellum railroad repair facility in the United States. For more than 100 years, this historic complex served as a major repair facility for the Central of Georgia Railway and was an important part of Savannah's industrial heritage. The Georgia State Railroad Museum is recognized as a National Historic Landmark District and has been designated by the State Legislature as the Georgia State Railroad Museum. Visitors can tour rail cars, see a roundhouse in action and enjoy children's activities at this historic site.

# FOR HISTORY BUFFS

## Battlefield Memorial Park

*Louisville Road and Martin Luther King, Jr. Boulevard  |  912.651.6825  |  chsgeorgia.org*

Located at the corner of Louisville Road and Martin Luther King, Jr. Boulevard, the **Battlefield Memorial Park** offers a thoughtful memorial to 800 soldiers who fought and died for freedom during the Revolutionary War. On October 9, 1779, more than 8,000 troops from three different armies clashed in the Battle of Savannah, the second bloodiest battle of the Revolutionary War. A monument now sits on top of what is left of the original Spring Hill Redoubt, with 800 Georgia granite stones representing those who died or were wounded during this legendary battle.

## Fort Pulaski National Monument

*U.S. Hwy. 80 East  |  912.786.5787  |  nps.gov/fopu*

Fort Pulaski National Monument, an historic 1847 fort located between Savannah and Tybee Island, played a key role during the Civil War, when Union troops bombarded this Confederate fortification with rifled canons. Tour this landmark brick fort for insight into American history. Fort Pulaski offers daily interpretive programs including guided tours and musket firings. Expanded living history programs, including hourly cannon demonstrations, are held each Saturday. This 5,700-acre facility, which is operated by the National Parks Service, also has extensive walking trails on site.

## Green-Meldrim House

*14 W. Macon Street  |  912.233.3845  |  stjohnssav.org*

The Green-Meldrim House overlooking Madison Square served as the headquarters for Union General William T. Sherman's posh headquarters during the Civil War in 1864. This spectacular mansion stands apart as one of the finest examples of Gothic Revival architecture in the United States and is located adjacent to St. John's Episcopal Church, which operates the mansion as its parish house. General Sherman wrote his legendary telegram presenting Savannah as a Christmas present to President Abraham Lincoln from a bedroom at this exquisite estate. Originally built for cotton merchant Charles Green, this home's Gothic Revival style includes stunning arched windows, sandstone parapet edging and intricate wrought iron detailing.

## King Tisdell Cottage

*514 E. Huntingdon Street  |  912.234.8000  |  kingtisdell.org*

For an overview of the city's African-American history, don't miss the King Tisdell Cottage, a restored Victorian structure that now serves as an African-American heritage museum. Built in 1896, this quaint cottage showcases exhibits focusing on Savannah and the neighboring sea islands, with an emphasis on African-American history. Highlights at the King Tisdell Cottage include rare artifacts like an original bill of sale for slaves written in Arabic by plantation slaves.

© *Bryan Stovall*

## Old Fort Jackson

*1 Fort Jackson Road  |  912.232.3945  |  chsgeorgia.org*

Protecting Savannah from invasions by sea, **Old Fort Jackson** has the distinction of being the oldest standing brick fortification in Georgia. Originally built in 1808, this National Historic Landmark is one of only eight "Second System" fortifications built prior to the War of 1812 still standing in the United States. The fort protected Savannah during the War of 1812 and served as the headquarters for the Savannah River defenses during the Civil War. Today, Old Fort Jackson offers military exhibits, daily cannon firing demonstrations during the summer and a serene environment with stunning views of the Savannah River.

## Wormsloe Historic Site

*7601 Skidaway Road  |  912.353.3023  |  gastateparks.org*

Georgia's oldest plantation, Wormsloe Historic Site brings the past to life. Wormsloe's photogenic 1.5-mile entrance features a majestic avenue lined by more than 400 live oak trees draped with Spanish moss. This 822-acre site offers the only standing architectural relic in Savannah that dates back to Georgia's founding. The tabby ruins of the home of Noble Jones, one of the original colonists who arrived in Savannah with General James Oglethorpe in 1733, offers a glimpse into the lives of Georgia's earliest British settlers. Wormsloe also features a Colonial Life area, displaying typical outbuildings on the property and providing information about the gardens and crops grown at Wormsloe in the 18th century. ❀

© Bryan Stovall

© Bryan Stovall

# Their Soul To Keep

*by Jessica Leigh Lebos*

FROM HAUNTED TOURS TO HISTORIC HEADSTONES, SAVANNAH'S CEMETERIES ARE ALIVE WITH INTRIGUE.

Their residents may be six feet under, but above ground, Savannah's historic cemeteries boast some of the most compelling scenery in the nation. Notable historical figures, war heroes and the occasional ghost can be sought among hand-cut grave markers and luxuriant foliage, giving visitors plenty of reason to commune with Savannah's dead and buried.

Within walking distance of other downtown sites is Colonial Park, stretching across six acres and accessed through a tall gate at the corner of Oglethorpe and Abercorn Streets. The city interred its prominent citizens here from 1750 to 1853—steamship magnate William Scarborough has a marker here, as does Button Gwinnet, one of the signers of the Declaration of Independence—though the majority of the graves are unmarked. Many rich symbols are inscribed in the headstones; many feature trees whose height represents the length of the deceased's life. Also be on the lookout for poppies (symbolizing death's long sleep,) overturned hourglasses and ominous-looking scythes. It's also a favorite stop on ghost tours.

Savannah's most famous final resting place is Bonaventure Cemetery, occupying a scenic spot on the Wilmington River just east of town. Created in the mid-1800s on the site of a former plantation by the same name, many visitors come to Bonaventure because of its association with the best-selling novel, *Midnight in the Garden of Good and Evil* by John Berendt. Photographer Jack Leigh's iconic image on the cover of *Midnight* features a statue known as the Bird Girl, which used to stand over the Bonaventure grave of Lucy Boyd Trosdal but has been moved to the Telfair Museum of Art in downtown Savannah. Famous residents include Revolutionary War patriot Noble Wimberly Jones, crooner Johnny Mercer and poet Conrad Aiken.

Established by the city as an annex to the Bonaventure grounds in 1933, Greenwich Cemetery is worth a visit to experience its tranquil gardens and river bluff views. Full of ancient statuary and exotic plant life, these 65 acres were once home to one of the most majestic privately held estates in the South, of which an elegant white marble fountain, a few outbuildings and a small pond remain as reminders of the past.

Laurel Grove Cemetery North and Laurel Grove Cemetery South don't get nearly the amount of visitors as Bonaventure, but these sprawling 150,000 acres on the western edge of the city provide a far-reaching serenity. As you traverse the grounds, be on the lookout for the huge Gettysburg section, with over 700 Confederate burials from the Civil War, and "Baby Land," a collection of tiny statues dedicated to Laurel Grove's youngest residents.

Split into northern and southern sections in the 1800s, white Savannahians were traditionally buried in Laurel Grove North and black Savannahians in Laurel Grove South. At least 24 Savannah mayors rest in the north section, alongside nine Civil War Generals, one U.S. Supreme Court Justice, Girl Scouts of America founder Juliette Gordon Low, "Waving Girl" Francis Martus and "Jingle Bells" composer James Pierpont. Established in 1853 as a dedicated burial place for slaves and "free persons of color," the south section provides eternal rest to many of Savannah's prominent African-American leaders, including First African Baptist minister Andrew Bryan. A major revitalization took place of Laurel Grove South in the 1970s, led by civil rights activist W. W. Law.

Privately owned and maintained by the Catholic Diocese of Savannah, the Catholic Cemetery is tucked away past Skidaway Road on Wheaton Street. Bucolic and off the beaten path, these oak-filled acres contain the remains of many of Savannah's Irish citizens, including members of the Confederate Army's Jasper Greens. Still active, it serves as an important site to the city's strong Irish heritage and history.

Situated on a forgotten strip of land near two freeways off West Boundary Street, the Old Jewish Burial Ground stands behind tall concrete walls. Established in 1733 by Mordecai Sheftall from land granted to him by King George II of England, the small cemetery contains the graves of some of the earliest founders of Mickve Israel, the third-oldest Jewish congregation in the country. ✿

© Bryan Stovall

**"Most Haunted City in America"**
– *CNBC.com*, October 2010

**"Top 10 Spookiest Cities in the World"**
– *MSN.com*, October 2010

*Opposite, left:* Colonial Park Cemetery happens to be one of the prettiest parks in town. *Opposite, right:* Angels are among the gravestones at Bonaventure Cemetery. *Above, bottom:* Laurel Grove Cemetery is the city's largest and also one if its most peaceful final resting places.

© Bryan Stovall

# A Walk Through History

SCATTERED THROUGHOUT A CITY LAYOUT UNLIKE ANY OTHER,
GLORIOUS SYMBOLS OF SAVANNAH'S UNIQUE PAST AND FLOURISHING FUTURE ABOUND.

*by Heather Grant with excerpts by Laura Clark*

Once upon a time there was a coastal bluff above a river that flowed steadily towards the Atlantic Ocean. In 1733, when General James Oglethorpe arrived on the scene, he not only built a colony in the name of England's King George II, he also transformed the area into one of the world's most beautiful cities.

Today, more than 250 years later, Savannah's one-of-a-kind squares and expansive public parks, along with the historic monuments featured throughout them all, give visitors a glimpse of days gone by and the spirit that continues to carry the city forward.

**Washington Square.** Nearly in sight of the Savannah River, Washington Square (named after America's first president) is bright and sunny and boasts an impressive array of tulips and daffodils in the spring. In the early 1900s, the locale was the primary staging area for huge New Year's Eve bonfires and was long known to locals as "Firehouse Square" thanks to a once-neighboring station.

**Warren Square.** Bordered by subdued clapboard houses in neutral hues, this square was named for Revolutionary War hero and Battle of Bunker Hill casualty Continental Army General Joseph Warren and is just the place to stop for a spot of shade on your way to the river.

**Reynolds Square.** Near bustling Broughton Street, Reynolds Square offers everything needed for a perfect evening out. On the southeast corner of this square you'll find the historic and sparkling Lucas Theatre built in 1921. Walk a few steps to the west of the square and you will discover The Olde Pink House, a favorite fine-dining institution housed in a building that dates back to 1771. And if the night's revelry has you in need of some moral alignment, look no further than the center of the square, where a monument stands to John Wesley, the founder of Methodism and a one-time rector of Christ Church of Savannah.

© Bryan Stovall

© Savannah Theatre

**Johnson Square.** This sprawling spot of land by the city's gilded capitol building is host to an obelisk dedicated to General Nathanael Greene. In 1901, the Revolutionary War hero's body was removed from nearby Colonial Park Cemetery and re-interred beneath the monument—so be sure to tip your hat to one of Georgia's great defenders as you pass.

**Ellis Square.** It wasn't long ago that Ellis Square was but a parking lot for downtown day-trippers, but following an extensive construction project that moved the lot underground and out of sight, the square is a revitalized and renewed showcase. The new festive fountains provide a wet place to play by day and a colorful light show at night, and this friendly space is presided over by a statue dedicated to lyrical legend Johnny Mercer.

**Franklin Square.** Named for founding father Benjamin Franklin, this square sits next to Vinnie Van Go-Go's, one of the city's favorite locales for a sizable slice of New York-style pizza. At one time housing the city's water tank, Franklin Square is now home to a monument honoring the Haitian volunteer soldiers that helped defend the city during the Revolutionary War's Siege of Savannah.

**Liberty Square.** At one time, this quaint square was as sizeable as the rest but renovations to nearby Montgomery Street resulted in the smaller Liberty Square that stands today. Though smaller than most, the square still displays a glorious rainbow of blooming azaleas in the spring.

**Telfair Square.** This square is named for three-time Georgia Governor Edward Telfair and his daughters, Mary and Margaret. In 1886, the Telfair family opened their home to the public as an art museum and school, which continue to thrive on the edge of the square. Be sure to stop by neighboring **Jepson Center for the Arts** for excellent exhibitions of 20th and 21st century art.

**Wright Square.** In the heart of beautiful Bull Street, Wright Square is bordered by charming court houses and boasts a monument to Central of Georgia Railroad founder and Savannahian William W. Gordon. The square also has a memorial to Yamacraw Indian Chief and friend of the colonists, Tomochichi. Remember to tread lightly here: this locale was the first cemetery of Georgia's colonists, who were unable to move the bodies of their beloveds after establishing new sacred grounds.

**Oglethorpe Square.** Named after the founder of the colony of Georgia, Oglethorpe Square has plenty of benches, making it the perfect place to get a lasting look at the façade of the **Owens-Thomas House**, one of the city's most exquisite house museums.

**Columbia Square.** With tall, pruned bushes and an ornate fountain at its center, Columbia Square is as elegant as the expansive homes and buildings that surround it, which include the Kehoe House, an opulent (and reportedly haunted) inn, and the **Davenport House Museum**.

**Greene Square.** Quiet and lush with tall trees and subtle landscaping, this mostly residential square is adjacent to two unique and antique crooked little houses—see if you can spy them.

**Crawford Square.** In a primarily residential neighborhood, Crawford Square brings locals outdoors with an appealing gazebo and basketball courts. Be sure to stop by neighboring Colonial Park Cemetery, among the oldest burial grounds in the country and the final resting place of Button Gwinnett, one of the only signers of the Declaration of Independence to meet a violent end.

**Chippewa Square.** Some may know this busy Bull Street setting as "Forrest Gump Square" since its eastern end was indeed the location of the bench scenes of the Academy Award® winning movie. Bordered by the bright lights of the historic **Savannah Theatre**, where professional singers and dancers perform family friendly musical shows, and the perfectly pleasant Gallery Espresso coffee house, the square is centered around a statue of General Oglethorpe keeping watch over all that happens here.

**Orleans Square.** Accented gracefully by the bubbling German Memorial Fountain, Orleans Square commemorates the War of 1812 victory of the Battle of New Orleans and is within sight of the Savannah Civic Center.

© Old Town Trolley Tours, Inc.

*Opposite:* Savannah's founder, General James Oglethorpe, keeps watch over his inventive grid city from Chippewa Square. *Above, left:* Johnson Square near City Hall hosts large celebrations and pays tribute to Revolutionary War hero, Nathanael Greene. *Above, right:* The historic **Savannah Theatre** is one of America's oldest operating live theatres and offers a year-round calendar of performances that combine music, dancing and a healthy dose of comedy. *(see ad page 51)* *Left:* Visitors pass by the First African Baptist Church on Franklin Square during a tour from **Old Town Trolley Tours**. *(see ad page 31)*

**Elbert Square.** Like Liberty Square, Elbert Square no longer boasts the size or glory of its former years but the stretch of land that does remain is a perfect place to rest before or after an evening spent at the nearby Civic Center.

**Pulaski Square.** Tall trees with outspread branches create a delightful canopy affect in quiet Pulaski Square, named for Count Casimir Pulaski, who perished during the Revolutionary War's Siege of Savannah.

**Madison Square.** As a busy tourist favorite, Madison Square gracefully brings the past and present together with its historic bordering buildings. The Greene-Meldrim House hosted General Sherman's headquarters when the Union Army took Savannah during the Civil War. Nearby is the popular Sorrel-Weed House, thought to be highly haunted and offering tours daily. And be sure not to pass up the city's finest little bookshop, E. Shaver Booksellers, situated behind the Hilton Savannah DeSoto Hotel.

**Lafayette Square.** In the splendid shadow of the Cathedral of St. John the Baptist and enhanced by a refreshing fountain, Lafayette Square is the perfect place to be on a lazy Sunday afternoon. Close to the **Andrew Low House** (former home to Juliette Gordon Low, founder of the Girl Scouts), this square is also within sight of the exquisite Hamilton Turner Inn, which was the first home in Savannah to boast electricity.

**Troup Square.** Bordered by closely trimmed hedges and containing a large sphere with heavenly symbols known as an "astrolabe", Troup Square is also home to the Unitarian Universalist Church of Savannah, known as "The Jingle Bells Church," where former organist John Pierpont, Jr. is thought to have composed the beloved holiday tune in 1857.

**Whitfield Square.** Quiet and romantic, this square's simple white gazebo and surrounding ornate Victorian houses make Whitfield Square a favorite wedding location for locals and visitors.

**Calhoun Square.** The income from Savannah's early 1800s cotton exports allowed Savannahians to build impressive houses along this shady square, which is situated next to the dazzling and imposing Wesley Monumental Church. If you're a fan of John Berendt's *Midnight in the Garden of Good and Evil* (or the accompanying film) be sure to stop into the nearby "The Book" Gift Shop.

**Monterey Square.** As one of Savannah's most photographed locations, Monterey Square is home to the infamous Mercer House, the main setting of the all-too true *Midnight in the Garden of Good and Evil*. After peeking inside this literary locale on one of the home's daily tours, venture across the park to see the Gothic-style Congregation Mickve Israel ,which, founded in 1733, houses one of the oldest Jewish congregations in America.

**Chatham Square.** Close to Forsyth Park and discreetly residential, Chatham Square (named for William Pitt, the Earl of Chatham and British Prime Minister) is hugged by Greek-revival homes that are certain to transport you to another time.

© Bryan Stovall

*Left:* Whitfield Square's white gazebo and the Victorian homes that surround it make this a popular wedding spot.

## MONUMENTS

Throughout Savannah's parks and squares you will find monuments that vary in appearance but collectively pay homage to the city's distinctive history. While most can be observed in the heart of downtown, there are others that find their home in not-so-obvious locales but are well worth discovering. Here we have listed these additional monuments and encourage you to visit *savannahga.gov* and click on the *squares, monuments, parks and cemeteries* button to find out more.

**African American Monument** (*Rousakis Plaza, River Street*)

**Anchor Monument to Chatham County Seamen** (*River Street, head of Abercorn Street*)

**Big Duke Alarm Bell** (*Oglethorpe Avenue near Fire Department Headquarters*)

**Bishop Henry McNeal Turner Monument** (*At Northeast side of Fahm & Turner Streets*)

**Button Gwinnett Monument** (*Colonial Park Cemetery*)

**City Exchange Bell** (*Bay Street, east of City Hall*)

**City Hall Rotunda Fountain**

**The Cohen Humane Fountain** (*Victory Drive median at Bull Street*)

**The Cotton Exchange Fountain** (*Bay and Drayton Streets*)

**Generals Bartow & McLaws' Busts** (*Forsyth Park*)

**Hussars Memorial** (*Emmet Park*)

**Irish Monument** (*Emmet Park*)

**Jasper Spring's Marker** (*Augusta Avenue*)

**Jewish Cemetery Marker** (*Oglethorpe Avenue*)

**The Myers Drinking Fountain (*replica*)** (*Troupe Square*)

**Oglethorpe Memorial Bench** (*Yamacraw Bluff*)

**Police Officers Monument** (*Oglethorpe Avenue*)

**Semiquincentenary Fountain** (*Lafayette Square*)

**St. Andrews Monument** (*Oglethorpe Avenue*)

**World War I Memorial** (*Victory Drive*)

**World War II Memorial** (*River Street*)

**The Washington Guns** (*Bay Street*)

**Yamacraw Bluff Marker** (*Bay Street - west*)

## PARKS

In most cities, you may think that the terms "parks" and "squares" are interchangeable but in Savannah, they represent two very distinctive meanings. Savannah's historic squares are located exclusively in historic downtown and typically occupy a width of only two blocks on each of their four sides. By comparison, the city's parks are both considerably larger and can be found in both downtown and midtown locations. Though differences do exist, one thing remains the same: the beauty and immaculate landscaping of these natural green spaces are certain to take your breath away!

### Emmet Park

Named for an Irish patriot and orator, Robert Emmet, Emmet Park is twice the width of most downtown squares and stretches for nearly five blocks down the east end of Bay Street. With its close proximity to the Riverfront, the park not only offers visitors an expansive green lawn, perfect for strolling, resting and playing, but also beautiful views of the Savannah River below. Once an Indian burial ground, the park is now home to several monuments including those to the German Salzburgers, the Celtic Cross, Savannah's fallen soldiers from the Vietnam War, the Chatham Artillery Memorial and the Old Harbor Light.

### Forsyth Park

Among Savannah's most recognized icons – and second only, perhaps, to the famous Bonaventure Bird Girl statue - is that of the gleaming Forsyth Park Fountain. This immense grand fountain is at the heart of Savannah's version of Central Park and was designed to resemble the grand fountain in Paris at the Place de la Concorde. Any day of the week, the 30-acres of Forsyth Park are alive with activity, from a casual game of frisbee, to the rhythm of joggers circling the park's one-mile perimeter. Originally donated to the city by William Hodgson (a private citizen), the park was later expanded in 1851 and officially named after then Georgia Governor, John Forsyth. In addition to its natural appeal, Forsyth Park also contains several monuments including that of the Confederate Soldier, the Marine Corps Monument, and the Spanish-American Monument. Recent renovations to the park include the addition of a boutique-style café, a jumping water feature and grand center stage. Throughout the year, citizens and visitors alike bring their blankets and picnic baskets to the park to watch a range of musical and theatrical performances hosted by the City of Savannah, SCAD and others. Directly adjacent to the park's new additions you will also find the Fragrant Garden for the Blind where wrought-iron gates lead you into a floral fantasyland that is a true delight for all of your senses.

### Morrell Park

Located directly on Savannah's Riverfront is Morrell Park, which also happens to be home to the city's famous Waving Girl statue. In 1996, Savannah's Olympic Flame was also erected here to commemorate the yachting events that were held in the city's nearby coastal waters. Holidays such as St. Patrick's Day, New Year's Eve and July 4th, among others, always fill Morrell Park with packed audiences who are there to enjoy a variety of entertaining performances.

### Daffin Park

Named after the second chairman of the city's Park and Tree Commission, P.D. Daffin, this Savannah park is located in the area known as midtown. Flanked by Victory Drive and Washington Avenue on its north and south respectively and Waters Avenue and Bee Road on its east and west, Daffin Park is a hub of activity for visitors as well as local residents in nearby neighborhoods. Water fountains, an indoor gazebo and paved walking trail are just a few of the highlights of the park but it is perhaps most well known for its nearby neighbor, historic Grayson Stadium, which plays host to the **Savannah Sand Gnats** baseball team and hundreds of fans each season. ❋

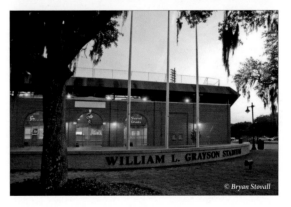

*Above, top:* The glorious Forsyth Park Fountain was designed to resemble the grand fountain in Paris at the Place de la Concorde. *Above, middle:* Home to many outdoor performances, Forsyth Park features an expansive center stage perfect for concerts that are open to the public. *Above, bottom:* Historic Grayson Stadium in Daffin Park is home to the **Savannah Sand Gnats** baseball team and has hosted such baseball legends as Hank Aaron and Babe Ruth. *(see ad - inside back cover)*

# Savannah's Flowers and Forecasts

FROM BLOSSOMS IN THE SPRING TO WEARING SHORTS IN WINTER, SAVANNAH'S SEASONAL SURPRISES ARE ALWAYS DELIGHTFUL.

*flowers by Jessica Leigh Lebos and forecasts by John Wetherbee*

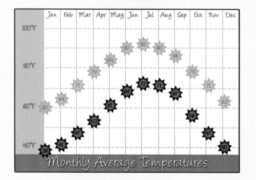

Monthly Average Temperatures

### 1. Camellias (December-February)

These dense, dark-leaved evergreen trees form pom-poms in late fall that burst into round, rose-shaped flowers throughout the winter. The flowers can be pink, red, yellow, white or variegated and come in single and double blooms. The most popular species found in Savannah gardens are Camellia japonica and Camellia sasanqua.

### 2. Azaleas (March-April)

Though it's impossible to predict exactly when it will happen, at some point in the early spring Savannah literally explodes with color, thanks to these ubiquitous shrubs. Filling the medians, sidewalks and squares with shades of purple, red, coral, white and pink, "Azaleamania" lasts for two to three weeks and usually coincides with several garden tours and festivals. It is truly a spectacle to behold!

### 3. Gardenias (May-June)

These heat-loving plants begin to put out highly fragrant flowers in early summer and often gear up for another bloom in late fall. The delicate, velvety white petals unfurl as a spiral and turn creamy yellow with age. Pluck one (with permission, of course) and float in a bowl of water to fill an entire room with a delightful scent.

### 4. Star Jasmine (May-July)

This clinging vine adorns Savannah's arbors, balconies and even mailboxes, throwing forth small, sweet-smelling clusters of white flowers during the early summer. Though often referred to as "Confederate jasmine," the evergreen is not native to the American South but to China.

### 5. Magnolias (June-July)

Each summer, these tall, stately trees with their waxy, brown-bottom leaves turn out white blossoms, infusing the air with a lemon-sugar scent. The bigger the tree, the larger the blossoms—some have the circumference of dinner plates!

### 6. Crape Myrtles (June-September)

The heat of summer brings out clouds of lavender, pink, maroon and white to fill the smooth gray branches of Savannah's many Crape Myrtle trees. After the tiny flowers peak, the leaves begin their own gorgeous showing of hues, turning shades of cinnamon red, dusty pink and mustard yellow before they fall and the trees begin another beautiful cycle. ❀

An integral part of any Savannah visit is getting outdoors, walking through squares, exploring hidden gardens and even venturing out onto the waters of our beautiful coastline. Experiencing all of Savannah's natural allure is, of course, best enjoyed when the weather is at its finest and while we may heat things up in the summer, on average you'll have every reason to seize the day with Savannah's inviting temperatures ready to greet you year round.

As a general rule, it's always best to start your day in Savannah early. Rains tend to be late in the day and the heat can become a little intense during the summer months for outdoor activities after lunch. All Savannah tour companies consider the weather when planning their tours and many schedules are built to enjoy Savannah during the most inviting times of the day.

If you're wondering what to wear in Savannah, comfortable shoes are definitely a must. In fact your whole suitcase might just consist of lightweight fabrics, unlined jackets, a hat and an umbrella. Other than something a bit dressier for a special dinner or a sweater first thing in the morning, when it comes to packing for Savannah, the weather is so pleasant it's just that easy.

It does get "cool" in Savannah at certain times of the year – even downright cold for a day or two. January is Savannah's coolest month but even so, the average afternoon highs still reach the 60-degree mark. There have been those rare occasions, however, when the city has been as cold as 3-degrees back in 1985 but the very next day it was up to 68 by the afternoon. Thanks to the effects of the nearby Atlantic Ocean, Savannah's cold snaps never last long. Speaking of winter, you may wonder if we've had any of the "white stuff" around here. We actually had a flake or two of snow last year but it melted as soon as it hit the ground. Historically, accumulations have occurred but, once again, the moderating waters of the Atlantic tend to keep snowfall to a minimum.

While snow may be a novelty in the low country, warm summers are a frequent visitor to the south. July tends to be the warmest month but it's also a great reason to seek out some fun "relief" on the beaches where the ocean's waters remain cooler than the air temperature. There have been triple-digit record setters in the past, some as hot as 105-degrees in 1986, but summer also brings Savannah's greatest average rainfall to cool things off, usually in locally heavy late-day thunderstorms.

Whatever time of year you visit, Savannah's weather is simply gorgeous with blooming springs that make way for an autumnal sanctuary. And just remember, if you ever find yourself in need of some shade, it doesn't get any better than a tall glass of sweet iced tea sipped on a breezy veranda with an overhead fan – just be sure to give a friendly wave and a "hi y'all" to anyone who passes by. ❀

TELFAIR ACADEMY
121 Barnard Street

OWENS-THOMAS HOUSE
124 Abercorn Street

JEPSON CENTER
207 W. York Street

TELFAIR
MUSEUMS

TELFAIR ACADEMY
121 Barnard St.

State Street

Telfair Square

Wright Square

Oglethorpe Square

OWENS-THOMAS HOUSE
124 Abercorn St.

York Street

JEPSON CENTER
207 W. York St.

art + history + architecture    912.790.8800    TELFAIR.ORG

©Richard Leo Johnson

©Bryan Stovall

# The Art Scene

GETTING LOST IN CENTURIES OF CREATIVITY AND ARTISTRY IS THE BEST WAY TO DISCOVER YOUR OWN.

*by Allison Hersh*

Georgia's First City warmly embraces the arts, nurturing emerging talent and celebrating visual creativity. With a range that encompasses everything from 18th century portraiture to black-and-white photography to wild multi-media installations, the entire city is a palette, inside and out.

In fact, the art scene has grown steadily over the last decade, anchored by the Savannah College of Art and Design's success and fueled by a growing appetite for original work by talented local artists. Today, art lovers can discover a wide array of styles, media and approaches that rival treasures found in established art meccas like New York or Santa Fe.

## MAIN ATTRACTIONS

Savannah's art museums are home to a number of world-class collections. From folk art to photography, visitors can enjoy something for every taste. Here are a few must-see stops for anyone with a passion for the visual arts.

### Jepson Center for the Arts

*207 W. York Street | 912.790.8800 | telfair.org*

This sleek glass-and-marble museum overlooking Telfair Square serves as the epicenter for contemporary art in Savannah. With galleries dedicated to Southern art, African-American art, photography and traveling exhibits, the Jepson Center delights art aficionados of all ages.

In addition, the Jepson Center also is home to a popular hands-on ArtZeum for kids, which includes commissioned works by glass artist Therman Statom and computer-video artist Daniel Shiffman. Children can learn about art through interactive, hands-on exploration, playing with a magnetic sculpture wall, building architectural structures with wooden pieces or experimenting with video art installations.

### Telfair Academy

*121 Barnard Street | 912.790.8800 | telfair.org*

Want to see the legendary "Bird Girl" statue that graces the cover of John Berendt's best-seller, *Midnight in the Garden of Good and Evil*? You'll find Sylvia Shaw Judson's iconic statue on permanent display at the Telfair Academy, where it had to be relocated after visitors overcrowded Bonaventure Cemetery, the Bird Girl's original location, in the wake of *Midnight's* success.

The oldest art museum in the South, the Telfair also features an impressive Sculpture Gallery, a dramatic Rotunda accented with works from the museum's permanent collection, and period rooms showcasing a world-class decorative arts collection with rare American and European antiques. Highlights from the permanent collection include stunning examples of American Impressionism, Ashcan School painting and the largest public collection of visual art in North America by poet Kahlil Gibran, best known as author of *The Prophet*.

### Beach Institute

*502 E. Harris Street | 912.234.8000 | kingtisdell.org*

This historic 1867 building, originally built to encourage African-American education in Savannah, houses an extensive collection of imaginative folk art by Ulysses Davis (1913-1990), a legendary Savannah woodcarver. The Ulysses Davis Collection, which is on permanent display at the Beach Institute, features a selection of sculptures by this self-taught African-American artist, including a complete collection of wooden sculptures devoted to each of America's Presidents.

Davis's sculptures have been featured at the Corcoran Gallery of Art in Washington, D.C., the High Museum of Art in Atlanta and the Library of Congress in Washington, D.C. Much of his work deals with spiritual themes and reveals a rich influence from African tribal art.

### SCAD Museum of Art

*Kiah Hall | 227 MLK Jr. Boulevard | 912.525.7191 | scad.edu*

Dedicated in 2002, the SCAD Museum of Art exhibits a wide selection of paintings, photography and mixed media work throughout the year. Showcasing nearly 4,500 objects, the museum is located in the former headquarters of the Central of Georgia Railroad, a restored 1856 Greek Revival treasure.

The SCAD Museum of Art features three major collections on permanent display: The Walter O. Evans Collection, which includes original work by African-American artists including Romare Bearden, Aaron Douglas and Jacob Lawrence; the Earle W. Newton Center for British and American Studies, which features 200+ paintings ranging from the early 17th century to the mid-19th century; and the Shirrel Rhoades Photographic Collection, which boasts 135 photographs by Ansel Adams, Annie Leibovitz, Karl Lagerfeld, Imogen Cunningham and Richard Avedon. ✿

*Opposite, left:* The modern lines of the **Jepson Center for the Arts** were designed by architect Moshe Safdie. *(see ad page 69) Opposite, right:* Peruse classic art at the **Telfair Museum**. *(see ad page 69) Above, top:* The Beach Institute displays the work of folk artist Ulysses Davis. *Above, bottom:* More than 4,500 works are showcased at the SCAD Museum of Art.

© Bryan Stovall, Ships of the Sea Museum

# Step Into History

HISTORY CAN BE SEEN AROUND EVERY CORNER IN SAVANNAH BUT IT IS BEST DISPLAYED
WITHIN ITS MANY IMMACULATE MUSEUMS.

*by Heather Grant*

Savannah's Southern charm is reminiscent of Antebellum days when ladies wore hoop skirts, gentlemen practiced chivalry and manners were the rule, not the exception. And while that era is certainly an important part of the city's past, its history dates back long before the war between the states to a time when most of North America had yet to be discovered and England was still considered home to most colonists. Thanks to the preservation efforts of generations of Savannahians and dedicated citizens, the city's intriguing 279-year history lives on within a myriad of museums that beckon you to travel back in time.

## MUSEUMS

### The Savannah History Museum

*303 MLK Jr. Boulevard | 912.651.6825 | chsgeorgia.org*

Housed within the former Central of Georgia Railroad passenger shed, the museum is adjacent to several others managed by the **Coastal Heritage Society**. Boasting more than 10,000 artifacts relating to early Georgia and coastal history, the exhibits include weapons dating back the Revolutionary War, a rare Native American dugout canoe, a fabulous display of women's hats and 20th century treasures like an Oscar® won by music man Johnny Mercer and the iconic bench used in the film *Forrest Gump*, filmed in Savannah.

### The Ralph Mark Gilbert Civil Rights Museum

*460 MLK Jr. Boulevard | 912.231.8900 | savcivilrights.com*

Within the former Wage Earners Savings & Loan bank built in 1914, three floors of interactive and photographic exhibits tell the story of the struggle and triumph of Georgia's oldest African-American community. Learn how the citizens of Savannah took Dr. King's philosophy of non-violence to heart and influenced city and business leaders to achieve equal rights during one of the most tumultuous times in our nation's history.

### Ships of the Sea Maritime Museum

*41 MLK Jr. Boulevard | 912.232.1511 | shipsofthesea.org*

The epic era of cross-Atlantic trade during the 18th and 19th centuries is given proper due at this exquisite museum housed in the elegant Scarborough House and its surrounding gardens. Handcrafted models of ships (including one of the first steamships to complete the Atlantic passage), exceptional paintings of maritime life and antiques hearkening back to a time when captains depended on the stars for nautical guidance make this a must-see for anyone who's ever had a dream of sailing adventure.

### Georgia Historical Society

*501 Whitaker Street | 912.651.2125 | georgiahistory.com*

Presiding over the northwest corner of Forsyth Park, stately Hodgson Hall has been home to Georgia's oldest cultural institution since 1876. Researchers and bibliophiles use this jewel of a library to examine its millions of manuscripts, photographs, maps and architectural blueprints for academic as well as genealogical pursuits. In addition to providing stewardship over Georgia history in the city where it all began, GHS also provides educational programming and publishes a magazine, *Georgia History Today*, and an academic journal, *Georgia Historical Quarterly*. The Society also has offices in Atlanta and manages thousands of historical markers throughout the state.

### Mighty Eighth Air Force Museum

*175 Bourne Avenue, Pooler | 912.748.8888 | mightyeighth.org*

Just minutes outside of downtown Savannah is the Mighty Eighth Air Force Museum, which honors the bravery and patriotism of the men and women of the Eighth Air Force. Though much of the museum is a journey back in time to the days of World War II, it also pays tribute to present-day members as well. Through its interactive exhibits, including a simulator of a B-17 bomber and a Combat Gallery filled with a fleet of restored aircraft that were used in battle, the Mighty Eighth Air Force Museum humbles and inspires all who visit. ❀

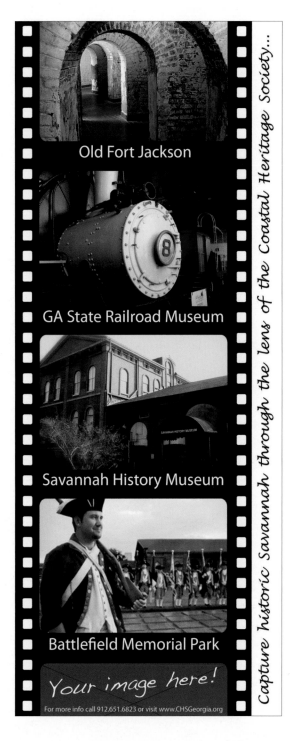

Old Fort Jackson

GA State Railroad Museum

Savannah History Museum

Battlefield Memorial Park

Your image here!

For more info call 912.651.6823 or visit www.CHSGeorgia.org

Capture historic Savannah through the lens of the Coastal Heritage Society...

© Bryan Stovall

# Soul Searching

## AN INSPIRATIONAL JOURNEY THROUGH
## SAVANNAH'S RELIGIOUS ROOTS

*by Heather Grant*

Savannah's first church service took place the very day General Oglethorpe docked his ship at the Yamacraw Bluff on February 12, 1733. It was attended by 120 new colonists and conducted by the general himself. Since then, Savannah's spiritual legacy has only gotten stronger and more storied.

Christ Church of Savannah may have been housed in different buildings throughout its history but it remains on the same ground that was designated by General James Oglethorpe himself in 1733. A young Anglican priest by the name of John Wesley, who would later found Methodism, served as rector of Christ Church from 1736-1737 followed by George Whitefield from 1738-1740.

As declared by General Oglethorpe, the colony of Georgia was established with the promise that any religion could be practiced—with the exception of Catholicism, a defense to the threat of then Spanish-occupied Florida. A few months after the colony's establishment, the English ship *William & Sarah* brought a group of 41 Jewish travelers, mostly of Portuguese origin, to Savannah. They became the Congregation Mickve Israel, still operating as the third-oldest congregation in the nation and occupying one of the country's only Gothic synagogues on Monterey Square.

Around the same time a few miles further north, the community of Ebenezer was established by 300 German-speaking Lutherans who came seeking religious refuge from their home country. The Salzburgers found freedom and as well as agronomic success, and their Jerusalem Church in Rincon stands as the oldest continuing Lutheran congregation in the country that still uses its original edifice.

Savannah is also home to America's oldest African American church, though two lay claim to the distinction: Both First African Baptist Church and First Bryan Baptist Church trace their roots back to Andrew Bryan, a baptized slave who founded the first ordained black Baptist church in

© Kevin Nightingale
© Bryan Stovall

*Opposite:* Housed in one of the only Gothic synagogues in the country, Congregation Mickve Israel has existed in Savannah since 1733. *Left:* The towering spires of the Cathedral of St. John the Baptist inspire awe as do the stained glass windows seen from the inside. *Right:* Christ Church of Savannah remains on the same ground that was designated by General James Oglethorpe himself in 1733.

1788. Following a schism over religious doctrine in 1832, the congregation split, with one group retaining the name and the other claiming the original building. The first white Baptist church was established in 1800, and the majority of churches in Savannah are affiliated with some type of Baptist denomination.

By 1799, the ban on Catholicism was lifted when the city granted permission for the construction of St. John the Baptist, back then a small church built to accommodate Savannah's increasing population of Irish immigrants. The stunning cathedral that stands today on Bull Street was dedicated in 1876.

The late 1800s saw the advent of a revival period that brought new religious interpretations such as Christian Science, Unitarianism and Mormonism, all of whom established local communities. The Jehovah's Witness and Pentecostal movements also found homes in Savannah during this time. Two new synagogues were also organized at the turn of the century, B'nai B'rith Jacob and Agudath Achim.

Also in the late 1800s St. John's Church emerged with its current building being consecrated to the service of God on May 7, 1853. Since that time, St. John's Episcopal has acquired the historic Green-Meldrim mansion as its Parish House, which was also once used as headquarters for General William Tecumseh Sherman of the Federal Army during the Civil War. It was from this house, in December of 1864, that Sherman sent his famous telegram to President Lincoln offering him the city of Savannah as a Christmas gift and sparing the city the same charred demise of so many before it.

The 20th century filled in any gaps in Savannah's roster of religious diversity. Large evangelical Christian congregations like Savannah Christian Church now thrive, as well as smaller groups practicing the traditions of Quakerism, Hindu, Buddhism and the Baha'i Faith. Savannah also has two mosques, the Islamic Center of Savannah and the Masjid Jihad.

Oglethorpe's vision of tolerance is a reality in Savannah. Not only do so many different faiths worship peacefully and respectfully, there is constant crossover of interfaith activities and support. Whatever you believe or whether you believe at all, there's no denying such a remarkable example of religious freedom. ❁

© Westin Savannah Harbor Golf Resort & Spa

# Sweet Tea to Green

FROM EXPANSIVE COASTAL VIEWS TO LUSH OAK CANOPIES, SAVANNAH'S GOLF COURSES PROVIDE A REFRESHING OUTDOOR ESCAPE.

*by Heather Grant*

Crisp in the fall, mild in the winter and spring, and sunny in the summer, Savannah's weather makes enjoying the outdoors a year-round pastime for visitors and residents alike. If you fancy yourself a golfer, then there's no doubt about it, you have arrived! Not only is the weather perfectly suited for this outdoor pastime, but Savannah also has a range of picturesque courses for every skill level and preference. So pull out your clubs and get ready to enjoy some of the best golf the south has to offer.

If you have reached Savannah via airplane, then you'll be pleased to know that your first golf opportunity is mere minutes from baggage claim. Crosswinds Golf Club, aptly named for its proximity to **Savannah/Hilton Head International Airport**, is a public course located at the airport exit near Interstate 95. Crosswinds' 18-hole championship course features an open parkland style design, while its Par 3 course offers the ideal opportunity to practice your short game. Crosswinds even illuminates its grounds for later play on selected weekdays during the fall and spring.

Once in Savannah, just across the river is Hutchinson Island, which is home to The Westin Savannah Harbor Golf Resort and Spa and its course, **The Club at Savannah Harbor**. Each year, this Troon Golf® course plays host to the PGA TOUR's Champions Tour Liberty Mutual Legends of Golf, a new Savannah tradition that brings out fans by the thousands to see true legends of the game up close and in person. "We welcome all of our visitors to play where the pros play," commented Dana Schultz, general manager, The Club at Savannah Harbor. "Our course invites all skill levels to experience exceptional course conditions with five sets of teeing areas and our professional staff is dedicated to delivering personalized service for all guests." This 18-hole daily fee resort course is dotted with water features, immaculate landscaping and a one-of-a-kind view of Savannah's towering Talmadge Bridge. Named a Top 100 of America's Golf Courses by *Condé Nast Traveler*, The Club at Savannah Harbor delivers the same amount of first-class care to its greens as it does to those who play them.

Keeping with the island theme, The Wilmington Island Club, which opened in 1927 and was designed by Donald Ross, is a public 18-hole course located just about 20 minutes outside of downtown Savannah. Its grand plantation clubhouse is the perfect welcome to this truly South-

ern course, decorated with towering oaks dripping with delicate Spanish moss and beautiful water glimpses throughout. In addition to its 18-hole course, The Wilmington Island Club also features a 30-tees driving range, perfect for those afternoons where you may not have time for a full 18 but definitely want to stay in the swing of things.

Throughout the Savannah area there are also several residential communities that boast spectacular golf opportunities. While most are private courses, there are opportunities for the visiting public including those at Henderson and Southbridge. The Henderson Memorial Course is located just off of Highway 204 near Interstate 95 on the southside of Savannah (accessible via interstate, it is approximately 25 minutes from downtown Savannah). This 18-hole municipal golf course also features a 22-tees driving range. Travel a bit to the west of Savannah and you will be on your way to the community and course of Southbridge. With its direct-exit route from downtown onto Interstate 16 West, you will reach Southbridge within 15 to 20 minutes of the Historic District. This popular community features many amenities, one of which is its 18-hole public golf course and 25-tees driving range.

Other public courses in Savannah include Bacon Park, which features three unique courses, the Live Oak, Magnolia and Cypress, The Hunter Golf Course, which is part of the military facility of Hunter Army Airfield, and the Mary Calder Golf Club with its nine-hole course directly adjacent to downtown Savannah on West Lathrop Avenue.

While you may hear more about sweet tea than tee times when you're out and about in the Historic District, there's no doubt that among Savannah's many passions, golf is certainly one of them. So if the weather is fine and you've got the time, tee up and play through, we guarantee even if your score isn't the best, you'll still take home fond memories of your Savannah golf experience. ❈

© Savannah Quarters Country Club

*Opposite:* While your focus may be on sinking a putt, the saltwater marsh and river views found at **The Club at Savannah Harbor** are always a welcome distraction. *(see ad page 77)* **Above, bottom:** Residents and their guests at Savannah Quarters can enjoy the challenges of this Greg Norman Signature Course along with the natural serenity that is all around.

# I Do Love *Savannah*

FROM CASCADING OAKS TO COASTAL VIEWS, SAVANNAH IS THE PICTURE-PERFECT SPOT TO SAY "I DO." *by Heather Grant*

© *Bryan Stovall, Forsyth Park*

For most brides to be, plans for a magical wedding day started long before the groom ever entered the picture (sorry guys).

The fairytale included many details no doubt but among them were a romantic spot where all those daydreams would come true. With its beautiful squares, horse-drawn carriages, grand historic churches and – of course – the beach, Savannah and surrounding areas are increasingly among the top picks for savvy brides who want it all on their special day.

As any new bride can attest, a wedding requires months of planning – depending upon the size of the event. So once you have selected your date and set your sights on Savannah, the next item to choose is location. Savannah has many historic and grand churches and some have open-door policies, meaning they are not exclusive to congregation members only, but you'll want to check with the church you're considering to be sure. Of course Savannah's picturesque squares are also a very popular location for your special day and can be reserved through the city, but keep in mind that the most popular squares may also be attractions for uninvited guests and traffic so touring your top picks ahead of time is always wise. Then there are the city's many interior locations and from major hotels to quaint B&Bs and banquet facilities the choice is truly yours. Some specialty locations to also consider include the Mighty Eighth Air Force Museum with its grand atrium, the new Richmond Hill City Center offering a southern plantation-style atmosphere and the Tybee Island Wedding Chapel, which offers a nostalgic Lowcountry feel in a new Tybee Island venue.

With the location set, your décor will likely be the next item to check off of your planning list. Savannah is home to many planning and rental companies who specialize in helping you create a look to reflect your special day. Classic Party Rentals often works with brides to be as well as businesses and offers a variety of rental items from table settings to chairs, linens and more. Savannah Special Events by Ranco offers full-service party and tent-rental services including dance floors and lighting as well as the essentials such as table settings, linens and more.

With tables reserved now it's on to the food. Creative Catering offers more than 16 years of experience serving at events that range from 50 to 5,000. For full-service facilitation, linen rentals, ice sculptures and more, Paul Kennedy Catering will work closely with you and your planner to achieve your dream results. The highly trained team at SAVOR... SAVANNAH Catering is also well known for its inventive dishes that are as beautiful as they are delicious.

Of course another charming facet of having a Savannah wedding is your mode of transportation. Whether you choose the romance of a horse-drawn carriage for two, the whimsy of a bicycle-style pedicab or the nostalgia of Savannah's trollies, you and your groom, or your entire guest list, can get from ceremony to reception with ease.

And last but certainly not least, you'll want to be sure to capture the moments of your Savannah wedding for a lifetime of memories. Savannah has fast become an epicenter for all things creative and that includes photography. Wedding photographers in the area have long abandoned the days of stoic and staged poses for candid shots that reveal the true essence of your wedding day. Whoever you choose, with Savannah as your backdrop you're sure to compile an album that is truly breathtaking.

With its natural beauty and destination appeal Savannah's popularity as a wedding venue means that you have countless professionals to call upon for your special day. We encourage you to visit *SavannahIDo.com* for a comprehensive listing of Savannah wedding professionals to make your wedding planning as romantic as it is effortless. ❦

## "Top 10 Romance Destinations in the U.S."
– *TripAdvisor.com*, May 2010

## "Most Romantic Getaways"
– *US Airways Magazine*, February 2010

## "Top Romantic Southern Escapes"
– *Southern Living Magazine*, January 2010

© Angela Hopper Photography

*Above:* With the bustle of River Street below you and the Savannah River stretching out before you, **Vic's on the River** is a picturesque spot for your wedding reception - and first kiss! *(see ad page 15)*

# By the Light of the Moon

## Send the Sun to Bed and Simmer Through Savannah's Cool Night Spots.

*by Christine Lucas*

© Erin Adams Photography

The dimming of a Savannah day signals a changing of the guard. There is a hush that pours across the city as locals and visitors refresh themselves in anticipation of night. Darkness broken up by dots of amber light makes the Historic District feel like a forgotten sound stage. Notice, in the absence of a breeze, how the moss-covered branches look like props awaiting whatever drama might unfold below.

Maybe it's that eerie stillness that sends many to start their evenings in the city's roof-top bars. These chic venues give you a chance to wear that something special you tucked in your suitcase. Start with Perch, located at 1110 Bull Street, on top of the celebrated restaurant Local 11ten. This sophisticated establishment is just outside the fray, and perfect for those who want comfortable seating where they can sip and chat. Be sure to try their *basil gimlet*, a deliciously simple mix of gin, basil, and lime juice.

**Rocks on the Roof**, is located on top of the Bohemian Hotel at 102 West Bay Street. It has the elegance that you'd expect from a luxury hotel overlooking the Savannah River. Their drink selection is wide enough to suit everyone in your party, and a tasty tapas-style menu tastes even more so when paired with the fresh air.

Craft beer enthusiasts must head over to The Distillery at 416 West Liberty Street. It is housed in what was once the Kentucky Distilling Company and is now owned by the Volen family whose signs boast, "No crap. Just craft." A wide variety of beers on tap and menu items flow throughout the restaurant's menu daily. "We carry 21 craft beers on tap daily – always rotating our selection," says general manager and Beer Guru Ben Volen. "Pairing beers with food, and allowing customers to try new things is the best part of the job," he adds.

The Crystal Beer Parlor, located at 301 West Jones Street, also resides in a building with rich history. John Nichols, who shares ownership with his brother, Phillip, has strong memories of visiting this eatery as a child. His father would sometimes leave him in the car while he went in and fetched a to-go order. "I knew when I saw that brown paper bag with the grease spots we'd be eating well that night," John says. The original Crystal Beer Parlor opened in 1933, and locals fell in love with the crab stew, burgers, and thick fries. A section of suds called "Beers of Our Fathers" includes classics like Ballentine XXX and Guinness Cream Ale. Dare take a sip, and your old man will show up shouting at you to mow the lawn.

© Bryan Stovall , Savannah's River Street.

Since beer is what's on tap so far, we encourage you to continue your journey down hops lane and visit **Moon River Brewing Company**. As the name may have indicated, this is an honest-to-goodness brewery where you can dine with a view of the restaurant's own brew tanks. With at least six original brews on tap each day, Moon River Brewing Company is anything but ordinary and serves a delicious menu of some of beer's favorite foods including hearty burgers and finger licking barbecue as well as items for vegetarians and vegans.

Savannah's Wild Wing Cafe, at 27 Barnard Street, also wants you to feel at home in the South. They have specials every night of the week and make a habit of hosting very cool bands. Their *mile high nachos* will take you back to days when your wallet was light and your mood lighter. Party with them at night, and then come back for their Blue Jeans Brunch which includes Southern classics like chicken and waffles for those who overindulged the night before.

Andy Homes, owner of Churchill's Pub & Restaurant, knows the look of a bar is what gives a place its character. That's why he had his built in England and brought over – with other authentic fixtures – on a ship. "It's important to me that people have a great meal, a great time and leave satisfied," says Andy. Their *bangers & mash* and *slow roasted beef with Yorkshire pudding* are comfort foods perfect for when there is a chill in the air (it does happen here, on occasion) plus the kitchen is open 'til 1 a.m., making them perfect for starving night-owls.

Of course, Savannah doesn't always flaunt its fine establishments. Tucked away on the corner of Broughton and Barnard Streets you'll find Jazz'd Tapas Bar. Once you see the Gap, you know you're close. Take those side stairs underground for martinis and live music (Tuesday thru Sunday). During Happy Hour (Monday thru Thursday, 4-7 p.m.), you'll find yourself enjoying the funky-meets-industrial vibe of the bar, but you will, no doubt, stay for the 35 tapas selections easily shared with friends.

Those looking for a romantic spot must head to Circa 1875 located at 48 Whitaker Street. An intimate pub sits beside a Parisian bistro where reservations are required due to the limited space. The French cuisine combines simple ingredients so perfectly that one must savor every bite. An extensive wine list compliments the delicious dishes you are sure to enjoy here.

With so much to experience, you'll never be able to fit it all in one night, so go ahead, raise your glass and toast to coming back to Savannah for more! ❀

© Paul Camp, Red Clover

© City Market, Art Center at City Market

# shop|savannah

# A Shopping High

IN BETWEEN YOUR TOURS OF OLD
BE SURE TO SHOP FOR SOMETHING NEW.

*by Angela Hendrix*

Upon arriving in Savannah, it only takes a few moments to realize this is a shopping paradise. From River Street to Broughton Street, throughout the Historic District and beyond, Savannah has something to offer every taste, preference and whimsy.

**Savannah Riverfront**

Start your journey on the historic Savannah Riverfront. As you survey the beautiful waterfront, take the opportunity to stroll by and visit the area's many stores. You'll find Savannah books, Civil War artifacts, Southern gourmet selections, nautical art, T-shirts, art galleries, antiques and more.

**City Market**

The four-block area in Savannah known as **City Market** is a must stop for those visiting Savannah. The mercantile and produce offerings of yesteryear in Savannah have been replaced by an eclectic blend of art galleries and specialty shops. Shoppers will discover unique gifts, original works of art and a host of other delights at the many shops and boutiques. One very unique feature of City Market is **The Art Center** where you can watch artists create original works of art in their studios. City Market is the perfect spot for delightful browsing or to just take a seat and relax in the courtyard shade.

### Broughton Street

A short walk from City Market and you'll find yourself on the revitalized and oh-so-chic Broughton Street. This street offers shoppers the unique opportunity to purchase everything from contemporary furniture to specialty made honeys to new and vintage items from around the world. Broughton Street is a mecca for furniture, interiors, clothing boutiques, antiques, art galleries and more.

### Downtown Design District

Woven through a portion of the Historic District, the Downtown Design District includes boutiques, apparel and antique stores as well as art galleries. Located mostly on Whitaker Street and its side streets, these stores offer wonderful home décor and items including furniture, art, gifts, antiques, bath, bed, interior, lighting and more. Make sure you seek out the specialty stores that offer you an intimate look and feel of Savannah's history, present and future.

### South Savannah

Venture out of the Historic District and you'll find just as much shopping. Abercorn Walk and 12 Oaks Shopping Center offer national and local retail options. Savannah also has two malls, Oglethorpe Mall and Savannah Mall, where anchor department stores and national brands abound.

From stores you already know to Savannah finds you will never forget, you are sure to experience the best of retail therapy right here. Just plan ahead and bring a big suitcase with 'lots of extra take-home room (you're going to need it!) – happy shopping! ❅

*Opposite:* Lather up to the handcrafted soaps at Nourish. *(see ad page 85)* *Top, left:* It's always a good day to shop in Savannah. *Bottom, right:* Broughton Street in Savannah is the perfect spot for brand names and specialty boutiques.

# HEAD-TO-TOE
# SAVANNAH
## STYLE

WHATEVER YOU FANCY, FROM HANDCRAFTED BAUBLES TO NAME-BRAND DESIGNERS, LET THE SHOPPING BEGIN!

*by Angela Hendrix*

Any woman, man or child shopping for clothes and accessories in Savannah is sure to find a fabulous chic experience!

**For children's clothing...** visit Sara Jane Children's Boutique, 202 East 37th Street, in the Historic District. Offering hip and unique items, Sara Jane carries Petunia Pickle Bottom, Tea Collection, Vineyard Vines, Mud Pie, Zuccini, Bailey Boys, and more in newborn to size 8 for girls and boys. While you shop, your little ones can play in their dress up box, enjoy a tea party, play in their pint-sized tent or sashay down their runway. Another fun stop for the children is **Del Sol** on River Street. They are the brand leader of color-changing apparel. Adults and children alike will love their T-shirts, shorts, nail polish, hats, jewelry and more. Also visit Punch & Judy, 4511 Habersham Street, a Savannah boutique focusing on clothing, accessories and baby gear since 1946. Other children's clothing and accessories stores include Just for Baby, Pollywag, Gymboree, Children's Place and more.

**For the gentlemen...** Savannah offers a wide selection of men's clothing. On Broughton Street, Marc by Marc Jacobs, features his ready-to-wear collection. Banana Republic and The Gap offer casual and business clothing as well as bags, belts, shoes, ties, hats and scarves. For local flair, you'll want to visit James Gunn on Broughton Street. They carry stylish and oh-so-chic clothing and accessories for men and women. And since 1972, J. Parker Limited has been providing fine apparel and sportswear to Savannahians emphasizing brands that signify not just luxury, but an ethic of quality-made goods and classic, timeless fashion.

Half-Moon Outfitters on Broughton Street is a great stop for men and women. Browse the huge selection of men's clothing including outerwear, sweaters, thermal tops, bathing suits and men's accessories for all your outdoor adventures. They carry The North Face, Patagonia, Chaco Sandals, Mountain Hardwear and more.

**For women...** there are endless possibilities for shopping. That's why Red Cover co-owner Leah Lancaster loves being located in Savannah. "I love shopping in downtown Savannah because it has many locally owned shops, from clothing stores to antique stores to art galleries, along with the historic beauty that the city offers. You can always find something unique in Savannah."

So start your shopping experience with Red Clover, located at 244 Bull Street. With the newest looks at affordable prices, Red Clover offers fun and unique prices that make your look come together in a relaxed, no pressure atmosphere. They have a wide selection of clothing, accessories and gifts from indie and local designers. Voted Best Fashion Value Boutique and Runner Up as Best Boutique of Savannah by *Savannah Magazine*, you'll find all your fashion needs at a price that's perfect for your budget.

The heart of shopping in Savannah, Broughton Street, features several women's clothing stores. We've already mentioned James Gunn for the men but make sure you check out their collection of women's clothing, swimsuits and apparel as well. Other stores you'll want to put on your list include Gaucho, which also has a Bull Street location, Terra Cotta, located behind Broughton on Barnard Street and Fab'rik, a shop-o-holic's dream. Fab'rik, 318 West Broughton Street, delivers high style all priced under $100 except for the extensive denim collection.

Savannah is also home to several consignment stores. Civvies, offers new and recycled styles as well as Cherry Picked Con-

signments, which carries high-end designer name consignments including Anthropologie, White House|Black Market, Lilly Pulitzer, Chico's, Marc Jacobs, Michael Stars, Tory Burch, Banana Republic, Trina Turk, Nanette Lepore, Lacoste, T-Bags, Diane von Furstenberg, BCBG, Juicy Couture and more.

On Whitaker Street, you'll find a cluster of shops that include The James Hogan Store, which opened in Savannah in 2004. The store carries Hogan's entire collection as well as renowned European and American lines such as Etro, Piazza Sempione, Max Mara, Rani Arabella, Lafayette 148, Pink Tartan, Magaschoni and Wolford. Mint Boutique features the hottest and most up-and-coming designers from New York, California and Europe, and Trunk 13 carries women's apparel, accessories and shoes that are fashion forward and reasonably priced.

Make sure you head down Abercorn Street into Savannah's midtown area for even more must-see shopping. At Abercorn Walk, an open-air shopping center, you'll find Ann Taylor Loft, Palm Avenue, a Lily Pulitzer store, White House|Black Market, and Talbots among others. Directly across from Abercorn Walk is the 12 Oaks Shopping Center, which is home to a variety of shops including a Savannah original, BleuBelle Boutique. BleuBelle is consistently voted Best Women's Store by *Connect Savannah* and Best Boutique by readers of *Savannah Magazine*. It was also honored with the Savannah Area Chamber's "Small Business of the Year" award. At BleuBelle Boutique, you'll find designers such as Diane von Furstenberg, Tory Burch, Milly, Ella Moss, Halston Heritage, Alice + Olivia, Michael Stars, 7 for All Mankind, Joe's Jeans and more.

Savannah also includes two malls. Savannah Mall, 14045 Abercorn Street, includes Dillard's, Burlington Coat Factory, Bass Pro Shops Outdoor World and Target. While the Oglethorpe Mall, 7804 Abercorn Street, has a Sears, JCPenny, Belk, Macy's and more.

# SHOP MY SAVANNAH

{ savannah's local guide to all things shopping. }

**shop***my***savannah**.com

*email* jaclyn@shopmysavannah.com 🐦 shopmysavannah 📘 shop my savannah

**For accessories...** visit Satchel on Broughton Street. This unique boutique specializes in designing and construction of custom leather goods including bags, purses, clutches, cuffs, portfolio cases and more. Zia on Broughton features an array of sterling silver and gold jewelry, exclusive accessories and home interior accents, which hail from numerous different designers from around the globe. They also offer a broad range of colored gemstones and unique, handcrafted pieces and handbags featuring modern and classic designs.

**And finally – shoes...** – that is, after all, what women really love! Savannah has many places to choose from when looking for shoes. The Globe Shoe Company has been a Savannah tradition since 1892. They feature footwear and accessories by Stuart Weitzman, Donald Pliner, Cole Haan, Sam Edelman, VanElli, Thierry Rabotin, Gentle Souls, Munro, Jeffrey Campbell, Ugg, Ecco, Mephisto and Think! Also visit Copper Penny, featured in *Lucky, In Style, Oprah* and *Cosmopolitan* magazines, and Savannah Shoe Company, offering the most comfortable, stylish, affordable and versatile shoes.

So grab a coffee, put on your comfortable shoes and start your Savannah shopping adventure! ✤

# THE QUEST FOR CASH

Even in today's credit-card culture, there are still those times when you just need some old-fashioned cash. Thankfully, you will find a number of ATMs throughout the historic district for just such a need. Here, we have provided a listing of those ATMs and their locations so when the urge to buy strikes, you can happily seize the day.

| | |
|---|---|
| **Ameris Bank** | 300 Bull Street, Suite A *(Hilton Savannah DeSoto)* |
| **Bank of America** | 22 Bull Street *(Johnson Square)* |
| | 2 W. Bay Street *(Hyatt Regency Savannah)* |
| | 255 Montgomery Street |
| **BB&T** | 7 E. Congress Street *(Johnson Square)* |
| | 201 W. Oglethorpe Street |
| | 1 International Drive *(Savannah International Trade & Convention Center)* |
| **Capitol City Bank & Trust Company** | 339 Martin Luther King, Jr. Boulevard |
| **The Coastal Bank** | 18 W. Bryan Street *(Johnson Square)* |
| **First Chatham Bank** | 111 Barnard Street *(Telfair Square)* |
| **First Citizens** | 13 E. York Street |
| **Regions Bank** | 15 Bull Street |
| **Savannah Bank** | 25 Bull Street *(Johnson Square)* |
| **Sea Island Bank** | 120 Drayton Street |
| **Suntrust** | 33 Bull Street *(Johnson Square)* |
| | 306 W. St. Julian Street *(City Market)* |
| **United Community** | 24 Drayton Street, Suite 100 |
| **Wells Fargo** | 136 Bull Street *(Wright Square)* |
| | 301 W. Oglethorpe Avenue *(Savannah Civic Center)* |

# Something Old, Something New

**From vintage antiques to stylish accents,**
Savannah's stores are filled with treasures for you and your home. *by Heather Grant*

Whether your style is antique or eclectic, **visitors to Savannah fall in love with the city's wide-ranging architecture and decor** and long to take a piece of that signature look back home. If you're one such visitor, you're in luck! Shops and boutiques old and new throughout Savannah offer customers selections that range from vintage to modern for the irresistible chance to own a stylish Savannah keepsake.

## HOME DÉCOR

### 24e
*24 E. Broughton Street | 24estyle.com*
As you walk through the doors of 24e, you may feel as if you've stepped out of Savannah and into a chic Manhattan design showroom. The good news is, thanks to the vision of 24e's owner, Ruel Joyner, you can enjoy all of that big-city sophistication right here in historic Savannah. As you browse the two levels of furnishings for every room in your home, including rugs, accessories and one-of-a-kind collections, let your shopper's high take over and just remember, they will gladly ship your purchases to you.

### Circa Lighting
*405 Whitaker Street | circalighting.com*
Let's shed some light on the shopping subject, shall we? Circa Lighting began in Savannah in 1998 and today offers customers a vast array of original lighting, lamp and accessory designs that impart the perfect balance of form and function. Stores are located in Savannah, Atlanta, Georgia, Charleston, South Carolina and Houston, Texas.

### Clipper Trading Company
*201 Broughton Street | clippertrading.com*
By working with independent artisans, Clipper Trading Company is able to offer customers the chance to own unique pieces that also promote humane working conditions and economic sustainability. Within its large showroom you will find the elegance of the Orient in imported Asian antiques, artifacts, furniture and crafts.

### DC2 Design
*109 W. Broughton Street | dc2design.com*
For a look that is both elegant and sophisticated, look to DC2 Design. Based out of Los Angeles, California, DC2 offers contemporary styles that incorporate the latest design trends, from lighting to furniture to accents and beyond, within its striking retail showroom.

### No. four eleven
*411 Whitaker Street | numberfoureleven.com*
You know those items you see and you think to yourself, "Where did she get that?" Just one visit to No. four eleven and you will have your answer. This quintessential downtown design shop offers a chic collection of furniture, accessories, linens, gifts and so much more perfect for that special find that will always remind you of your Savannah experience.

### The Paris Market and Brocante
*36 W. Broughton Street | theparismarket.com*
Paris comes alive in this glorious retail recreation filled with whimsical finds. Self described as a "storehouse of treasures" you will delight in the two levels of merchandise for every room in your home (and some just for you) brought to Savannah from international destinations including London, Milan, Rome, Hungary, Holland and of course, Paris.

## ANTIQUES

### 37th at Abercorn Antiques and Design
*201 E. 37th Street | 37aad.com*
The sheer size will tell you that this is one location where you will quickly lose all track of time. Encompassing six city blocks and 7,000 square feet of antiques, 37th at Abercorn Antiques and Design is filled with items from the past as well as designs born of the present including furniture, lighting, collectibles, jewelry, art, rugs – and so much more.

### Jere's Antiques
*9 N. Jefferson Street | jeresantiques.com*
Room after room, floor after floor, if you love to search for those amazing antique finds, then Jere's is a must on your list. For more than 35 years, Jere's has provided customers with an extensive collection of rare English and Continental furniture from the 18th, 19th and 20th Centuries as well as a range of decorative pieces. This 33,000 square-foot showroom is sure to delight and intrigue all who enter.

### Peddler Jim's Antiques
*526 Turner Boulevard | peddlerjims.com*
Like a page out of a novel, Peddler Jim's is the type of antique store where you'll find treasures and an experience to write home about. For more than 35 years, Jim has sold jewelry, china, furniture, lighting, books, art, toys, military items and more with an inventory he has gathered from estate sales and antique shows throughout the southeast. As his website indicates, if the fishing is good, he may not be tending shop so it's best to call ahead.

### Pinch of the Past
*2603 Whitaker Street | pinchofthepast.com*
Specializing in home accents as well as restoration of historic and vintage pieces, Pinch of the Past is a step back in time where you'll discover items to cherish far into the future. From salvaged ceiling medallions to one-of-a-kind hardware, even custom castings and high-quality reproductions, you'll have as much fun searching for your favorite find as you will taking it home.

### Savannah Antique Mall
*1650 E. Victory Drive*
Just minutes outside of the heart of downtown on Savannah's world-famous Victory Drive you'll find the Savannah Antique Mall. The "mall" portion of the name is the result of the multiple dealers who set up shop here selling everything from home furnishings to jewelry as well as collectibles, art and more.

### Wright Square Antique Mall
*14 W. State Street*
As you journeyed to Savannah, you likely had a vision of buying something a bit vintage and something a bit eclectic to remember your travels. Now you can find both all in one place at the Wright Square Antique Mall. Featuring the antiques and collectibles of more than 30 local dealers you will delight in the handpicked treasures that fill this store with whimsy and personality. ❧

© Bryan Stovall, Chroma Gallery

© SCAD, shopSCAD

"Top 25 Arts Destinations"
– *American Style Magazine*,
June 2010

"An American Best City
for Coffee"
– *Travel + Leisure*,
February 2011

# The Art of Shopping

*by Allison Hersh*

**WHATEVER YOUR HEART DESIRES, SAVANNAH'S GALLERY SCENE ELEVATES SHOPPING TO AN INSPIRING ART FORM.**

### The Art Center at City Market

*308, 309 W. St. Julian Street |*
*savannahcitymarket.com*

This is where creativity comes to life – literally! Within **City Market** you will find the unique opportunity to explore two levels of studio after studio featuring nearly 20 artists at work, breathing life into canvas, sculpture and so much more as you stand in awe. A full listing of artists can be found on the opposite page and as you'll see, the more time you can dedicate to this inspiring shopping experience, the better!

### Chroma Gallery

*31 Barnard Street | chromaartgallery.com*

From canvas to glass, jewelry and more, the mission of the Chroma Gallery is to "be a leader in the presentation and promotion of contemporary visual arts." Works from a multitude of artists can be purchased at Chroma, where they also host a visiting artist series throughout the year.

### Gallery 209

*209 East River Street | gallery209Savannah.com*

Housed in a renovated 1820s cotton warehouse on River Street, Gallery 209 offers those shopping for Savannah artistry two floors filled with pieces by local artists. Original works and limited-edition reproductions fill every space in this brick-and-beam exposed gallery and are sure to please the artist within you.

### Gallery Espresso

*234 Bull Street | galleryespresso.com*

One of the city's best venues for emerging artists, this bustling café serves as an excellent launching point for many local painters and photographers. A great place to catch a rising star and a cup of coffee.

### Red Gallery

*201 E. Broughton Street | scad.edu*

This showcase Savannah College of Art and Design gallery always has something interesting to see. Works by artists ranging from Rembrandt to Andy Warhol have been featured here, often alongside compositions by SCAD students, faculty and alumni. Exhibits rotate frequently throughout the year.

### Reynolds Square Fine Art Gallery

*31 Abercorn Street | reynoldssquarefineart.com*

Throughout this breathtaking gallery you will find paintings, sculptures, handcrafted wood workings and more, all created by artists who live in Savannah. Whether they were born here or now love calling Savannah home, the inspiration of this historic city is beautifully embodied in pieces for you to own and cherish.

### Sentient Bean

*13 E. Park Avenue | sentientbean.com*

This laid-back, free-trade coffee house features art exhibits year-round, many of which focus on themes relating to the environment, social justice and peace. An affordable community gallery with a conscience.

### shopSCAD

*340 Bull Street | shopscadonline.com*

This Savannah College of Art and Design gallery and boutique specializes in hand-crafted items, from mixed media to paintings to quilts, by SCAD students and alumni. With a wide range of prices, Shop SCAD serves as a great place to find creative, unique gifts. ❀

 # THE ART CENTER
## AT CITY MARKET

### City Market Art Center Studios *(912.232.4903)*

| | | |
|---|---|---|
| **Alix Baptiste** | 309 W. St. Julian St. - *Upper Level Studio FSU-1A* | 912.441.0845 |
| **Addiktspace Studios** *Nelson/Stavella/Larsen Art Studio* | 308 W. St. Julian St. - *Upper Level Studio FNU-106* | |
| **Albert Seidl** | 308 W. St. Julian St. - *Upper Level Studio FNU-110* | 912.665.1485 |
| **Brian MacGregor** | 308 W. St. Julian St. - *Upper Level Studio FNU-104* | 912.596.2201 |
| **Carl Kotheimer** **Goldeneye Gallery** | 309 W. St. Julian St. - *Upper Level Studio FNU-4* | 912.239.9977 |
| **Carrie L. Kellogg** **Photography Gallery** | 309 W. St. Julian St. - *Upper Level Studio 3* | 912.441.9020 |
| **Dennis Roth** | 308 W. St. Julian St. - *Upper Level Studio FNU-105* | 912.220.2234 |
| **Diane's Knitting Studio** | 308 W. St. Julian St. - *Upper Level Studio FNU-108* | 912.441.9020 |
| **Dottie Farrell &** **Bess Ramsey** | 309 W. St. Julian St. - *Upper Level, Studio FSU-1* | 912.341.0122 |
| **Eric Wooddell** | 308 W. St. Julian St. - *Upper Level Studio FNU-104* | 912.631.8250 |
| **Ga11ery 11** | 309 W. St. Julian St. - *Upper Level, Studio FSU-11* | 912.441.2093 |
| **Gallery 10 - Pamella Dykema** | 309 W. St. Julian St. - *Upper Level, Studio FSU-10* | 912.429.5326 |
| **Gallery 9 - Sue Gouse** | 309 W. St. Julian St. - *Upper Level, Studio FSU-9* | 912.667.4378 |
| **Kerry Harried** | 309 W. St. Julian St. - *Upper Level, Studio FSU-2* | 912.224.6925 |
| **King David** | 308 W. St. Julian St. - *Upper Level Studio FNU-107* | 912.441.9040 |
| **Luba Lowry** | 309 W. St. Julian St. - *Upper Level, Studio FSU-7* | 651.894.3053 |
| **Osibisa Fine Arts -** **William Kwamena-Poh** | 309 W. St. Julian St. - *Upper Level, Studio FSU-8* | 912.201.9009 |
| **Roeder Kinkel Studio** | 308 W. St. Julian St. - *Upper Level Studio FNU-109* | 912.332.9082 |
| **Susie Chisholm/Sculptor** | 309 W. St. Julian St. - *Upper Level, Studio FSU-6* | 912.441.6261 |
| **Wayne Chambers** | 308 W. St. Julian St. - *Upper Level Studio FNU-101* | 912.234.6899 |

*www.savannahcitymarket.com/art*

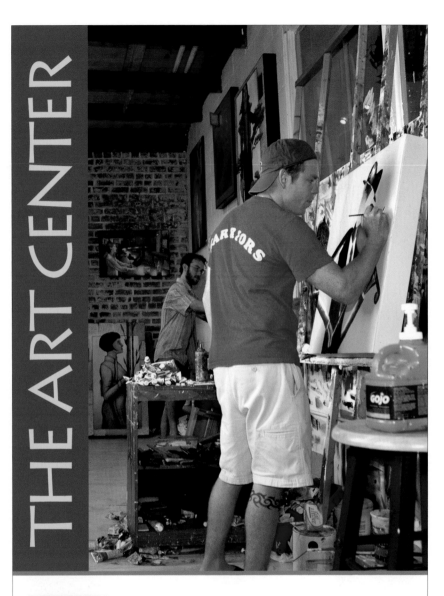

THE ART CENTER at City Market is a community of working artists who make and sell their work in a series of studios and galleries.

See 35 artists at work in the studio lofts.

912.232.4903 • SavannahCityMarket.com
309/315 W. St. Julian Street (upstairs)

# Southern Beauty

## From a Day at the Spa to Products that Pamper at Home, We Reveal the South's Best Beauty Secrets

*by Heather Grant*

© Magnolia Spa

As any good Southern lady will tell you, the secret to that youthful glow is – *well* – a secret. **When it comes to beauty in the south, it just comes *"naturally"* - or so everyone says.** Thankfully, we know better and we also know the best places in Savannah to seek out professional treatments for that youthful, supple, Southern glow and also where to buy tricks of the trade to take home with you.

### Spa Time

If you came to Savannah with a new pair of walking shoes, chances are, you broke them in on your first day. Seeing Savannah by foot provides visitors with one of the most in-depth views of this fascinating city, but it can also leave you in need of a relaxing day off. Across the river on Hutchinson Island inside the grand Westin Savannah Harbor Golf Resort and Spa, you'll find a little piece of Heaven, literally. **The Heavenly Spa by Westin** delivers pampering that is truly surreal, with a focus on promoting wellness during travel. As Savannah's largest spa, The Heavenly Spa by Westin includes 20 treatment rooms and, of course, all of those extras that are designed to make your experience absolutely divine. "With every treatment our clients also gain access to the full Club facilities including our workout room, locker room, robes, sandals, sauna, steam shower and more,"

commented Cindi Moreno, spa director. After your Heavenly treatment, you'll want to be sure to save some time to visit the spa's Sanctuary area where you can bask in your newfound relaxation while enjoying herbal teas, dark chocolates and complimentary mimosas.

On the east end of Savannah's Historic District you'll find the Savannah Marriott Riverfront with its **Magnolia Spa**. Here, the traditional massage, facial, manicure, pedicure and other popular treatments are performed in total relaxation including a unique service called a Balancing Ritual. This 80-minute healing treatment begins with a hand-applied massaging exfoliation treatment made from Indonesian ginger. After a steam shower and relaxing rinse, you are then enveloped in a cocoon wrap of Acai and Rice Peptide culminating in a soothing scalp massage and Eucalyptus foot massage to complete your calming experience. "Our clients definitely leave feeling energized with supple, conditioned skin that's smooth and glowing," commented Michelle Connor, spa director.

As you venture a few blocks from the heart of downtown and into the green expanse of Forsyth Park, you will also stumble upon the Mansion on Forsyth Park. This impeccably restored Victorian mansion is also home to the Poseidon Spa where, as its name suggest, many of the treatments take their cue from the ocean's natural healing abilities. For a dual relaxation and stretching experience,

© Magnolia Spa

© Nourish

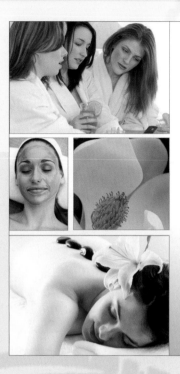

consider the Privai Aroma Thai Massage. With its blend of aromatherapy and Thai stretching techniques, you will enjoy a full sensory experience that leaves you utterly relaxed and restored.

In addition to spas found within Savannah's many hotels, you also have your choice of independent locations to choose from as well. Savannah Day Spa, which operates in a beautifully restored historic downtown home, is a full-service spa where the relaxation begins as soon as you enter its doors. If you find yourself shopping on Broughton Street and in need of a soothing treatment, Spa Bleu is located just off of the popular shopping area and their Rain Drop massage may be exactly the escape you need. Tucked away on Abercorn Street near East York Lane you will discover the Sweetwater Spa, which offers a sublime experience through massages, facials and a range of treatments for every customer.

A bit closer to Savannah's midtown area you'll find bliss at Glow MedSpa and Beauty Boutique, which features the newest and latest beauty services as well as a beauty boutique with products for sale from exclusive product lines. Glow's professional aestheticians are expertly trained to treat you to a full range of pampering services including massages, facials, oxygen treatments and much more so that you can achieve the boutique's promise to *find your inner peace and outer glow.*

Though Savannah itself may move at a fairly relaxing pace, no vacation is truly complete without a little pampering. So whatever spa you choose or treatment you select, just consider it all part of the truly laid-back Savannah way of life. Chances are, you could get used to this.

### PRODUCTS THAT PAMPER

Naturally *(pun intended)* keeping your skin radiant is the foundation to every beautiful look and that means a trip to **Nourish** is a must. This specialty boutique offers customers an indulgent selection of natural bath products including soaps, moisturizers, aromatherapy and even selections for baby. Be assured, this is not your ordinary soap. "Nourish features handmade natural body care products made from the best ingredients that Mother Nature has to offer," remarked Shoshanna Walker, owner. Not only is the natural appeal of Nourish intriguing but the way they market their products is as well with soaps sold by the bar, the slice, and in liquid form.

If you want that Savannah beauty to follow you home, then stop by See Jane Apothecary and Beauty Bar, the ultimate source for cutting-edge, independent and high-end beauty and grooming products. As you step into this beauty bar on Broughton Street you'll be instantly swept away by the extensive lines of hair care, body care, makeup and so much more in displays that are as attractive as the products will make you feel. See Jane also offers baby care, home accents and pet care in addition to luxury spa services such as facials, manicures, pedicures and makeup application.

While Savannah Bee Company may be famous for its honey, you will also love their oh-so-sweet offering of beauty products that will leave you feeling utterly delicious. Savannah Bee's showcase store is located on Broughton Street in Savannah and uses nature's golden goodness in a variety of edible pure honey products as well as in a full line of body care products including body butter, soap and lip balm – yum!

Truth be told, it really is what's on the *inside* that counts, but there's no denying that when your outside looks fantastic, you just feel better through and through. So go ahead, treat yourself to Savannah's beauty secrets because nothing makes you feel quite as good as a little personal pampering! ❀

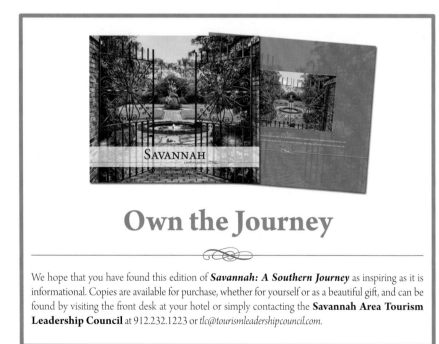

SAVANNAH

# Own the Journey

We hope that you have found this edition of **Savannah: A Southern Journey** as inspiring as it is informational. Copies are available for purchase, whether for yourself or as a beautiful gift, and can be found by visiting the front desk at your hotel or simply contacting the **Savannah Area Tourism Leadership Council** at 912.232.1223 or *tlc@tourismleadershipcouncil.com*.

© Bryan Stovall, Monterey Square

# History Meets High Tech
## with Savannah's Smartphone Apps

Not so long ago smartphones were a novelty but today, they are often viewed as necessity, especially when it comes to finding your way in a new city. Thankfully, there are those tech-savvy geniuses out there that have developed a variety of Apps to help Savannah's visitors (and even locals) hold the key to Savannah's best in the palm of their hands – literally. Below we have listed a few of the more popular options and invite you to make these high-tech helpers part of your visit to Savannah.

**Savannah Magazine: Best of the City.**
*savannahmagazine.com (look for the App link at the top of their home page)*
Let the readers and editors of Savannah Magazine introduce you to the best in local shopping, dining, nightlife, events and more with this free App.

**Tour Buddy.**
*tourbuddy.net*
This App is like having your own personal tour guide on your phone and delivers an interactive tour experience complete with suggested route information. Prices vary depending on the App you choose. Tour Buddy also encourages you to upload content to create your own Tour App.

**Savannah Now.**
*savannahnow.com/apps*
Get a digital replica of the daily paper plus the latest in Savannah events, local video and breaking news from the Savannah Morning News and savannahnow.com. Only $1.99 per month.

**St. Patrick's Day.**
*stpatsguide.com*
This Irish holiday is much more than a day in Savannah and thanks to the St. Pat's Guide App, now you can get information about planned festivals and more starting February 18 through March 20. At a cost of 99¢, the St. Pat's Guide App will also provide helpful tips to navigate the city during what has grown to be the second-largest St. Patrick's Day Parade in the world!

## DINE | SAVANNAH

| | | |
|---|---|---|
| 45 Bistro | 912.234.3111 | 123 E. Broughton Street |
| **700 Drayton**<br>*(Mansion on Forsyth Park)* | **912.721.5002** | **700 Drayton Street** |
| **17Hundred 90** | **912.236.7122** | **301 E. President Street** |
| Alligator Soul | 912.232.7899 | 114 Barnard Street |
| **Aqua Star**<br>*(Westin Savannah Harbor Golf Resort & Spa)* | **912.201.2085** | **1 Resort Drive** |
| B. Matthews Eatery | 912.233.1319 | 325 E.Bay Street |
| **Belford's Savannah**<br>**Seafood and Steaks** | **912.233.2626** | **315 W. St. Julian Street** |
| Blowin' Smoke BBQ | 912.231.2385 | 514 MLK Jr. Boulevard |
| Boar's Head Grill<br>& Tavern | 912.651.9660 | 1 Lincoln Street |
| **Café Zeum**<br>*(Jepson Center for the Arts)* | **912.713.6049** | **207 W. York Street** |
| The Chart House Restaurant | 912.234.6686 | 202 W. Bay Street |
| Churchill's Pub | 912.232.8501 | 13 W. Bay Street |
| **City Market** | *Please see page 39 for a full listing of City Market Dining* | |
| The Crab Shack | 912.786.7009 | 40 Estill Hammock Road |
| Crystal Beer Parlor | 912.349.1000 | 301 W. Jones Street |
| **Dolphin Reef**<br>*(Ocean Plaza Beach Resort)* | **912.786.8400** | **1401 Strand Avenue** |
| EatItandLikeIt.com | | |
| Elizabeth on 37th | 912.236.5547 | 105 E. 37th Street |
| **Fiddler's Crab House** | **912.644.7172** | **131 W. River Street** |
| Garibaldi's Café | 912.232.7118 | 315 W. Congress Street |
| GoWaiter.com | 912.335.5343 | |
| Huey's on the River | 912.234.7385 | 115 E. River Street |
| Jazz'd Tapas Bar | 912.236.7777 | 52 Barnard Street |
| **The Lady & Sons** | **912.233.2600** | **102 W. Congress Street** |
| Leopold's Ice Cream | 912.234.4442 | 212 E. Broughton Street |
| Local 11ten | 912.790.9000 | 1110 Bull Street |
| Lovin' Spoons | 912.355.2723 | 7400 Abercorn Street |
| The Melting Pot | 912.349.5676 | 232 E. Broughton Street |
| **Moon River**<br>**Brewing Company** | **912.447.0943** | **21 W. Bay Street** |
| The Olde Pink House | 912.232.4286 | 23 Abercorn Street |
| **The Pirates' House** | **912.233.5757** | **20 E. Broad Street** |
| **River House Seafood** | **912.234.1900** | **125 W. River Street** |
| **Rocks on the River**<br>*(The Bohemian Savannah Riverfront)* | **912.721.3800** | **102 W. Bay Street** |

| | | |
|---|---|---|
| **Ruth's Chris Steak House** | **912.721.4800** | **111 W. Bay Street** |
| Sapphire Grill | 912.443.9962 | 110 W. Congress Street |
| The Shrimp Factory | 912.236.4229 | 313 E. River Street |
| **Spanky's River Street Pizza**<br>**Galley & Saloon** | **912.236.3009** | **317 E. River Street** |
| Sticky Fingers Rib House | 912.925.7427 | 7921 Abercorn Street |
| **Tubby's Tank House**<br>**River Street** | **912.233.0770** | **115 E. River Street** |
| Tubby's Tank House<br>Thunderbolt | 912.354.9040 | 2909 River Drive |
| **Uncle Bubba's Oyster House** | **912.897.6101** | **104 Bryan Woods Road** |
| **Vic's on the River** | **912.721.1000** | **26 E. Bay Street** |
| Wet Willie's | 912.233.5650 | 101 E. River Street |
| Wild Wing Café | 912.790.9464 | 27 Barnard Street |

## EXPERIENCE | SAVANNAH

| | | |
|---|---|---|
| **Andrew Low House** | **912.233.6854** | **329 Abercorn Street** |
| **ArtZeum**<br>*(Jepson Center for the Arts)* | **912.790.8800** | **207 W. York Street** |
| Battlefield Memorial Park | 912.651.6825 | Corner of Louisville Road<br>and MLK Jr. Boulevard |
| **Coastal Heritage Society** | **912.651.6823** | **303 MLK Jr. Boulevard** |
| **City Market** | **912.232.4903** | **Jefferson at W. St.**<br>**Julian Street** |
| City of Savannah | | 2 E. Bay Street - City Hall |
| Classic Party Rentals | 912.927.2666 | 8115 Waters Avenue |
| **The Club at Savannah Harbor** | **912.201.2240** | **2 Resort Drive** |
| Club One/The Bay Café | 912.232.0200 | 1 Jefferson Street |
| Creative Catering | 912.341.3663 | |
| **Davenport House Museum** | **912.236.8097** | **324 E. State Street** |
| **Del Sol** | **912.236.6622** | **423 E. River Street** |
| The Fairways at<br>Savannah Quarters | 912.450.9876 | 101 King Fisher Circle |
| Garden City Convention<br>& Visitors Bureau | 912.966.7777 | 100 Central Avenue,<br>Garden City |
| **Georgia State Railroad**<br>**Museum** | **912.651.6823** | **601 W. Harris Street** |
| Hard Hearted Hannah's<br>Playhouse | 912.659.4383 | 35 Barnard St. Suite 300 |
| Historic Savannah<br>Carriage Tours | 912.443.9333 | 100 Aberdeen Street |
| **Historic Savannah**<br>**Foundation** | **912.233.7787** | **321 E. York Street** |
| HostSouth | 912.232.6373 | 249 E. Lathrop Avenue |

© Clive Barber, The Landings

# Savannah: *a southern journey* | directory

| | | |
|---|---|---|
| **Jepson Center for the Arts** | **912.790.8800** | **207 W. York Street** |
| **Juliette Gordon Low Birthplace** | **912.233.4501** | **10 E. Oglethorpe Avenue** |
| K Shuttle | 877.243.2050 | 2788 US Hwy 80 W. |
| Kelly Tours | 912.964.2010 | 2788 US Hwy. 80 W. |
| KeytoSavannah.com | 912.236.9539 | |
| **The Landings at Skidway Island** | **912.598.0500** | **1 Landings Way N.** |
| Liberty Mutual Legends of Golf | 912.236.1333 | 101 E. Bay Street |
| Mighty Eighth Air Force Museum | 912.748.8888 | 175 Bourne Avenue |
| **Old Fort Jackson** | **912.232.3945** | **1 Fort Jackson Road** |
| Oglethorpe Trolley Tours | 912.233.8380 | 215 W. Boundary Street |
| **Old Savannah Tours** | **912.234.8128** | **250 MLK Jr. Boulevard** |
| **Old Town Trolley Tours** | **912.233.0083** | **234 MLK Jr. Boulevard** |
| **Owens-Thomas House** | **912.233.9743** | **124 Abercorn Street** |
| Paul Kennedy Catering | 912.964.9604 | 1370 Hwy. 80 E. |
| Plantation Carriage Company | 912.201.9900 | 88 Randolph Street |
| Pooler Chamber of Commerce & Visitor's Bureau | 912.748.0110 | 175 Bourne Avenue |
| Richmond Hill City Center | 912.445.0043 | 520 Cedar Street, Richmond Hill |
| Richmond Hill Convention & Visitor's Bureau | 912.756.2676 | 520 Cedar Street, Richmond Hill |
| River Street Market Place | 912.220.9101 | 22 W. Bryan Street |
| **River Street Riverboat Company** | **912.232.6404** | **9 E. River Street** |
| Savannah.com | 843.757.9889 | |
| Savannah Book Festival | 912.358.0575 | 3025 Bull Street |
| **Savannah Children's Museum** | **912.651.6823** | **601 W. Harris Street** |
| Savannah Civic Center | 912.651.6550 | Corner of Liberty and Montgomery Streets |
| **Savannah/Hilton Head International Airport** | **912.964.0514** | **400 Airways Avenue** |
| **The Savannah History Museum** | **912.651.6840** | **303 MLK Jr. Boulevard** |
| Savannah International Trade & Convention Center | 912.447.4000 | 1 International Drive |
| **Savannah Music Festival** | **912.525.5050** | **216 E. Broughton Street** |
| Savannah Quarters Country Club | 912.450.2280 | 8 Palladian Way |
| Savannah Riverfront | 912.234.0295 | 404 E. Bay Street |
| **Savannah Sand Gnats** | **912.351.9150** | **1401 E. Victory Drive** |

| | | |
|---|---|---|
| Savannah Special Events by Ranco | 912. 944.6200 | 1200 W. Bay Street |
| **The Savannah Theatre** | **912.233.7764** | **222 Bull Street** |
| The Savannah Walks | 912.238.9255 | 37 Abercorn Street |
| Savannah Yoga Center | 912.232.2994 | 1319 Bull Street |
| SAVOR ... SAVANNAH Catering | 912.447.4000 | 1 International Drive |
| Segway of Savannah | 912.233.3554 | 102 E. Liberty Street |
| Ships of the Sea Maritime Museum | 912.232.1511 | 41 MLK Jr. Boulevard |
| **Telfair Academy** | **912.790.8800** | **121 Barnard Street** |
| Tour Services | 912.661.0964 | 104 Welch Street |
| Tybee Island Marine Science Center | 912.786.4289 | 1509 Strand Street |
| Tybee Island Wedding Chapel | 912.786.0054 | 1112 US Hwy. 80 |
| **Tybee Tourism Council** | **877.339.9330** | **802 First Street, Tybee Island** |
| Urgent Care of Historic Savannah | 912.234.3714 | 144 Lincoln Street |
| **Visit Savannah** | **877.SAVANNAH** | **101 E. Bay Street** |

## SHOP | SAVANNAH

| | | |
|---|---|---|
| 24 e | 912.233.2274 | 24 E. Broughton Street |
| **The Art Center at City Market** | **912.232.4903** | **309/315 W. St. Julian Street** *(upstairs)* |
| **City Market** | | *Please see page 39 for a full listing of City Market Shopping* |
| **Del Sol** | **912.236.6622** | **423 E. River Street** |
| **Heavenly Spa by Westin** | **912.201.2250** | **2 Resort Drive** |
| Levy Jewelers | 912.233.1163 | 101 E. Broughton Street |
| **Magnolia Spa** *(Savannah Marriott Riverfront)* | **912.233.7722** | **100 General McIntosh Boulevard** |
| **Nourish** | **912.232.3213** | **202 W. Broughton Street** |
| Red Clover | 912.236.4053 | 244 Bull Street |
| River Street Sweets | 912.234.4608 | 13 E. River Street |
| Savannah Antique Mall | 912.232.1918 | 1650 E. Victory Drive |
| Savannah Candy Kitchen | 912.233.8411 | 225 E. River Street |
| **ShopMySavannah.com** | | |
| Wright Square Antique Mall | 912.234.6700 | 14 W. State Street |

For more information on ***Savannah: A Southern Journey***, scan this code with your smartphone.

© Old Town Trolley Tours of Savannah, Inc., The Cotton Exchange

## PUBLISHER

### Tourism Leadership Council

Marti Barrow, *Executive Director*
Jaclyn Schott, *Marketing and Member Services Manager*
Leigh Anne DiVito, *Administrative Assistant*

## MANAGING EDITOR

Heather Grant

## CONTRIBUTING WRITERS

Jesse Blanco
Laura Clark
Angela Hendrix
Allison Hersh
Jessica Leigh Lebos
Christine Lucas
Buffy Nelson
John Wetherbee

## CREATIVE DESIGNER

Abigail Carter Gravino

## PHOTOGRAPHER

Bryan Stovall

## CONTRIBUTING PHOTOGRAPHERS

Erin Adams
Angela Hopper
Kevin Nightingale

Savannah accolades courtesy of Visit Savannah.

Published by the Savannah Area Tourism Leadership Council
www.tourismleadershipcouncil.com
P.O. Box 10010, Savannah, Georgia 31412

ISBN 978-0-615-56256-8
Printed in Canada